I0608267

Published by: Experimental Chapbook Press
Cover Design by: Experimental Chapbook Press

Library of Congress Control Number: 2021903952
ISBN-13: 978-1-7364310-0-9

Skip Rhudy

ONE PUNK SUMMER

Experimental Chapbook Press

Bands and song titles referenced are from the following recordings:

AC/DC, *Let There Be Rock*, Atlantic (1977)
Black Flag, *Damaged*, SST (1984)
Dicks, *Live At Raul's Club*, Rat Race Records (1980)
Fear, *The Record*, Slash(1983)
    More Beer, Restless (1985)
Hüsker Dü, *Zen Arcade*, SST (1984)
Ramones, *Ramones*, Sire (1976)
Sex Pistols, *Never Mind the Bollocks*, Warner (1977)
Violent Femmes, *Violent Femmes*, Slash (1983)
meatpiston, *random recordings*, unreleased, (2000)

For atmosphere these recordings are recommended listening before, during, and after reading.

© Experimental Chapbook Press
POB 2376
Seguin, TX 78156

For Mr. Meat, my good friend, *aber auch für Berliner Schriftsteller* Hans Christoph Buch.

ONE PUNK SUMMER

SKIP RHUDY

—Tony Lee hauled ass.

Down the darkening streets he pedaled, chunky mountain bike tires a-whirring, descending Exposition Boulevard hills, flying over concrete curbs twisting handlebars and hooting loud; he landed with a smashing clank; five more minutes to the store where he'd rendezvous with his friend, the Meat.

Mom and dad were out for an evening at Bass Concert Hall – Beethoven's Ninth.

Around a final corner, at the store, sprinkler mists smelling of wet grass from the golf course; Tony Lee grabbed the back brake hard and skidded sideways to a stop.

He hopped off and dropped his bike on the sidewalk.

A brightened row of windowpane welcomed him, papered with specials on vegetables, bread, and beef. Moms and dads pushed carts rattling madly with defective rubber wheels. Cash flowed and merchandise moved, a punk with a purple Mohawk stood by the windows, looking defiant inside. Tony Lee walked over to the doors and stopped. For a moment nothing happened, then the punk turned and Tony Lee saw that it was his friend. He could hardly believe his eyes.

Tony Lee went Meat, is that you?

The Meat laughed hard, spread his arms like a preacher, then thumped his chest and went hell yeah, dude, this is the new me!

—inside the store they laughed about that shock and bought two quarts of beer then got on their bikes and rode. The Meat jabbered, hooting and hollering at Tony Lee. He wore boots, a black leather jacket and jeans. Swerving down the street he turned sideways to show his new profile and went hey, what about this 'hawk?

Tony Lee went wow, how'd you do that?

The Meat went my friend Roxanne did it. Hey, you know what?

No, what?

The Meat went like, she plays drums dude. And, like, I told her hey I gotta friend who plays guitar. And she went like, wow, let's start a band.

Tony Lee went what?

The Meat screeched, thrusting his fist in the air.

Hell yes we're going to start a band dude. Like, we're gonna make a record.

Tony Lee thought that his friend had gone crazy.

So he went but Meat, I only know three chords.

Then the Meat went so what?

Tony Lee swigged more beer.

The Meat went listen, I already thought up a name for us. Wanna know what it is?

Tony Lee went sure.

The Meat went The Slash!

Tony Lee didn't say anything. They swerved down the street in the dark, and Tony Lee took another long swig of beer. Then he turned to his friend.

He went dude.

What?

Tony Lee went that name sucks.

The Meat burst out laughing and they clanked their big quart beer bottles together and started a chant:

We suck, we suck, we suck, we suck.

And then more laughter echoing in the neighborhood, kids voices in the distance, fading. Too much pedaling with too much beer – a gut full of suds – made Tony Lee feel like throwing up.

The Meat went listen, I got a song I wrote. Our first song. It's called *No More Nuthin'*. Wanna hear it?

Skeptical, Tony Lee went sure, I guess.

The Meat intoned distorted guitar licks:

Bah da da-da-da, bah da da
No more TV and no more news
No more Rock and Roll
No more blues
Bah da da-da-da, bah da da

No more black and no more white
No more color and
No more light

Hearing this, Tony Lee started laughing. He went shit man, even *I* could play that! The Meat laughed out loud and went but wait, there's more:

No more abortion and no more birth
No more people and
No more earth
No more, no more
No more nuthin!

The Meat shouted for all to hear: Every one of our songs under thirty seconds.

Tony Lee started laughing again. And up with the bottles. And sloshing back down. They brought them down, and foam spurted out of Tony Lee's bottle and ran over his hand and dribbled white rivulets downward and Tony Lee covered the hole of the bottle with his mouth.

The Meat went suck it, suck it.

They took another big swig, and more.

On they pedaled furiously around corners toward the house of Suzy Creamcheese, flinging away the empty bottles which arced twisting through the air and bounced somewhere on a lawn then shattered on a sidewalk in the dark. Then they were flying full speed down the big hill on West Lynn toward 6th street and suddenly the Meat shouted, and yanked his brake handles and skidded and Tony Lee skidded too and they both steered toward the curb, hopped it, and already they saw the people outlined in the light of the house. They dropped their bikes in the dust.

A lot of people stopped talking and looked at the Meat when he stomped up onto the old-school wooden porch. He seemed a beast of sorts; they were unsure of themselves.

The Meat went hey, where's the brew?

No one said anything at first and then someone went it's back there, dude, in the kitchen.

The Meat went hey, thanks.

Tony Lee followed the Meat through the house, followed the high 'hawk that cut the room, an axe blade slicing the whole into halves of staring faces.

8

Someone yelled hey Meat, what's with the haircut?

The Meat went this is the new me!

Someone went Jesus Christ, a freak.

Who said that?

No one spoke as the blade of the 'hawk turned back and forth scanning the still faces in the room.

That's what I thought went the Meat.

And then his boots heavy clomping on the wooden floor to the kitchen where he shouldered and bumped his way through the crowd at the beer keg and they all moved out of his way. Tony Lee was shocked. His friend, who had always been Meat-the-Meek, was suddenly acting like some kind of super aggressive asshole.

Two beers, went Meat to the boy at the pump.

Recklessly the boy went maybe you'd better wait your turn, friend.

For a moment no one spoke.

Then the Meat slowly twisted his head sideways, and abruptly started shaking his face blubbering cheeks and lips, teeth showing from inside out, spittle flying from his open pie hole all over the kitchen, spittle drooling to the floor. The people flinched back and the boy with the keg hose turned away, grimacing.

Jesus fucking Christ!

Black flexible tube was handed blindly to the Meat.

The Meat took it and roared. He turned his head back and he pressed the button and a stream of beer squirted into his open mouth. He filled it completely, let dribbles run down the sides of his face, then swallowed it all at once. He cackled insanely and burped.

Ahh. That's better. Now I'll take those two beers.

He gave the hose back to the boy, who decided it might be a good idea to just fill up their cups.

Beered up the Meat and Tony Lee stood alone in the crowded living room. Most the people had disco haircuts or long hair and stayed away from them, because they were scared of the Meat. So they stood by themselves talking until Suzy Creamcheese came over.

Suzy had broad horn-rimmed glasses from the fifties. She liked black leather and chains; tonight she wore a black leather mini-skirt, a white T-shirt, and black tights.

Suzy went hey wow, Meat, what a great 'hawk.

He went thanks Suzy.

The jacket's great too, went Suzy Creamcheese, touching the leather. Tony Lee saw what was happening, how Suzy was digging on his previously very shy friend the Meat, and suddenly he felt his jeans, *AC/DC* T-shirt, and Adidas were just not cutting it anymore.

Suzy Creamcheese went hey listen, have you guys seen that movie *Decline of Western Civilization*?

Together they went no.

She went it's a movie about punk in LA. There's this scene where the members of a band tell all about how they found a work-man guy dead in the backyard.

Suzy Creamcheese laughed nervously.

She went at first they just stood around looking at him.

She laughed nervous again.

Then they propped him up on his ladder and they left the body there overnight.

Suzy Creamcheese finished with a laugh.

Tony Lee went wow, that's fucking sick shit.

Suzy looked around the room and went hey wow, there's a lot of duds here right now. But they'll clear out when the fun people show up. Do you guys wanna hear my new *Fear* album?

The Meat went hey, all right, and they followed Suzy Cream-cheese to her room.

It was painted black and had aluminum foil pasted on the windows so that no light could get in during the day. There were clothes strewn everywhere.

She went hey guys, check this out.

While Suzy Creamcheese put a cassette in the tape player, the Meat found a pair of black leather panties on a dresser and held them up at Tony Lee. He made a crazy face, eyes popping out of his head, and lapped the air with his tongue. Now Tony Lee knew for sure his friend was wrong. The old Meat would never ever have done anything like that – he was way too introverted.

Then they were drinking beer listening to *Fear* and astounded as Suzy Creamcheese hopped and jumped around the room sing-ing the words to the *Fear* song *Beef Baloney* and Tony Lee and the Meat, inspired by the wacky gyrations of Suzy Creamcheese, started running wild around the room too, all three of them thrashing and drinking to mad images of flailing sexual debasement in song.

—out in the hall again, Tony Lee in a shredded and magic-markered T-shirt Suzy Creamcheese had given him (*that* shirt you have on just won't do, Tony Lee), and with a black leather studded belt; he was following Suzy and the Meat who suddenly was pressing her against the wall kissing her. Tony Lee was shocked at his friend's new self and slid past them into the blaze of the room; the whole place was supplanted; different people, different music; what had happened Tony Lee didn't know. And music he did not know either was playing loud, very loud – someone shouted it's *Hüsker Dü* man – and people were standing or thrashing, boots and jeans, jackets black.

The beer cups up and down, a platinum blond in the corner eying him and she looked mighty fucking hot, *Pink Turns To Blue* and Tony Lee got a beer from the keg and stood around, for him playing air guitar, jamming to the tunes.

Hey you.

Tony Lee turned to the shouting voice. It was that platinum blond girl who'd been looking at him.

Me?

She laughed, sparkling eyes and beauty.

Yeah, you. C'mere.

She took Tony Lee's hand in her little hand and pulled him down the hall, past where he'd left Suzy Creamcheese and the Meat, who weren't to be seen anymore, and this girl took him all the way to the end of the hall. She took Tony Lee into the bathroom, closed and locked the door, so that his heart felt suddenly queer beating against the walls of its cavity. She looked at him and went Suzy told me you liked crank.

Tony Lee went crank? What's that?

Christi laughed hard and went oh golly. I should have known Suzy was lying to me.

She pulled a small mirror out of her purse and a bag of powder and lumps of white. With a razor blade she cut the lumps into lines.

She went my name's Christi.

He went I'm Tony.

She went I know.

He went how'd you know?

'Cuz I asked Suzy.

Christi finished scraping the powder into lines and rolled up a bill and holding one nostril closed she snorted a line with someone pounding on the door yelling hey, hurry up.

She held the rolled bill to Tony Lee, who stared at it.

Tony Lee went I don't know. I don't ...

She went it's cool, and then snorted up the other line. Insta-rush boiling membranes in her nose with heat turning cool she smiled and leaned her head back, moaning a soft moan; Tony Lee looked at Christi's face. He thought it was a very pretty face and she had half-moon shaped eyes and smooth skin, her eyebrows black, that platinum blond hair touching her shoulders.

She went you know the party's getting better.

He went yeah.

She went there's a lot of fun people coming later.

She moved closer to Tony Lee but the door got pounded on again; some dude shouting hey come on, get a move on dammit.

Christi turned to the door and shouted back hey man, what the fuck? Can't a girl give a guy a blowjob in peace?

The people outside started laughing and then she started laughing and Tony Lee did too. Christi moved so close to Tony Lee that she pressed up against him. She looked right into his eyes. He thought something good was going to happen. Maybe right now.

Another loud bang on the door.

Someone went hey, come on, I really gotta go.

Christi looked momentarily at the locked door, and she went oh well fuck. And head shaking with disappointment she went okay Tony, let's go have some fun.

—there were a line of faces looking at them when they walked out like maybe they'd been doing nasty in the bathroom. Christi led him down the hallway and knocked on Suzy Cream-cheese's door and then busted in without waiting. There, the Meat on top, his white butt bare pumping and Suzy's legs up in the air – surprised the Meat and Suzy open-mouthed – so Christi shut the door.

Damn!

Christi giggled and took Tony Lee's hand again and started walking; she looked back at Suzy's door and Tony Lee wasn't sure but he thought she went wow I want to get laid too.

Soon he felt really drunk and saw her eyes all happy and shit and out in the living room more punks and Tony Lee saw the white foam fountain of a reverse chug spewing and sitting on the couch talking without stop to Christi ... it was Christi, wasn't it? And all he wanted was to learn that guitar lick, see her pink, *Hüsker Dü*—

Tony Lee not knowing whatever or what he was really going to do, but standing up, Tony Lee shouted hell yeah this is what I want, this is it, what time three o'clock Victor Hitler! Mom and dad I'm sorry. And the Meat clapping him on the shoulder holding a bottle of rum and shouting with the music and this was where he was heading in a way that couldn't be stopped and feeling the booze full in the blood with *Fear*, the Meat going I don't care about you—

Screaming right in Tony Lee's face fuck you and laughing like hell about it and then there was a slam and there he was, Tony Lee, floating in slow motion circles banging bodies and flying and as one unit drifting up seeing hair that stiff against the motion stood straight and later, sitting next to Christi talking to Butthole who went hey, dude, you need a new haircut.

And Tony Lee went all right.

And starting with scissors shearing away. A little bit of glue.

Tony Lee wanted more beer. Staggering to find the keg near empty dribbling foam. In the fridge a can of Colt 45. He took it and reeled down the hallway, and there she was, and wasn't he on the couch again with her? Slam the beer – pause for a puke. Tony Lee on hands and knees and he looked up to see the face of the Meat looking down who went ah hell, you're all right.

Staring at the floor Tony Lee panted and went yeah.

—rosy dawn spread her fingers across the sky, and Tony Lee had a punk hair cut, short spikes on top and buzzed close on the sides all around except in back they left a long skinny tail that hung down to one side, braided. And him, Tony Lee, sitting watching the sunrise the music still playing, waiting on the porch for a new day rising. Christi sat down next to him, swung her white skinny legs up and down.

She went hey, wasn't that cool?

He went sure.

She went all that music.

Her legs kicked high in Tony Lee's sight and he grabbed one and slid his hand up, across a bony knee over thigh and crick at the hip soft torso squeeze just under the rib cage that was expanding with the draw of breath, stopping at a small breast which he kneaded clumsily. And kissing wet, beer tainted tongues.

Curious, he stopped and went like, well, Suzy said you have a boyfriend.

She went of course I do. Doesn't everybody?

Then there was the sun and later Tony Lee fell asleep in the morning alone and he thought to himself seeing the sun he thought he knew how he wanted to live, it was this way, which was his and not theirs.

—ensconced in the shadows of his room under temporary house arrest, Tony Lee rolled around on his bed, alternately wrapped in sheets and bare, while erections came and went. Suddenly it was all about Christi, her happy self, her total confidence, her shining bright. And why couldn't he be like her? At the least he wanted to have that spirit, right now, wrapped around his naked body. Better her legs, he thought – then he felt a pained guilt that was not of his own making.

Tony Lee reflected everything he could remember about the party, which wasn't a lot. He remembered the Meat energetically singing songs. Beers. Suzy Creamcheese. Christi ... and some dude named Butthole?

Inspired, Tony Lee stood up. Playing air guitar he sang into an imaginary microphone. He pointed at the wall and went

I'll burn this house down

I'll sweep these walls with fire

Then paused ... trying to force something from nothing, he wanted a song to come out, but nothing did. He sat down on his bed again and put his head in his hands. If the Meat could do it, why couldn't he?

Tony Lee went because I'm a fucking idiot.

Intermittently Tony Lee strummed brainlessly his real guitar, a mangled mash of chords played clumsily.

He had to find a way to make up with his parents and get over to the Meat's. His parents had been so pissed when he finally came home that they'd instantly grounded him. Mom spoke the edict, while his dad, Victor Hitler, hadn't said a single word, sitting on the couch with his back to Tony Lee, reading a paper.

Mom went: What *did* you do to your hair, young man?

Before banishment he'd been taken to her bathroom where she'd clippered his cool punk haircut into a mangled kind of military-style crew-cut.

—at dinner Zeus fired his bolts.

Victor Hitler looked straight at Tony Lee. His bizarre mustache and his Führer-like silvery front comb-over would make Tony Lee laugh – if he'd only had the guts.

Victor Hitler went Tony, I'm afraid I have to ground you for the rest of this month and the next.

Tony Lee, outraged, slammed his fist down one the table and went two months? But that's the whole summer!

Victor Hitler went don't interrupt. You know you're not supposed to go to these sinful parties, and I don't want you drinking beer. But especially no drugs. No drugs at all.

Tony Lee blinked. He knew what was next: The Testament Speech. Victor Hitler started off as expected—

> *This world is a test of faith, Tony. It is not about ac-*
> *tion. We have to know our place in God's Creation*
> *and the path to true salvation. Self-denial and hard*
> *work will be rewarded not only now but also in the*
> *Hereafter.*

Give me the Olympians, Tony Lee thought. Always the same shit. But then something different after all:

> *And right now, Tony, you're in the Hereafter. As far*

*as those sick friends of yours are concerned you
are already dead. You* – Victor Hitler paused and
leaned in for effect – *you are now in the afterlife.*

Tony Lee went hold on. What do you mean?
I mean they can't reach you, and you can't reach them.
You mean I can't even talk to my friends on the phone?
Victor Hitler went that's right. For two months. No leaving
the house. No talking to your ... I mean these ... these *people.*
Victor Hitler expelled the last word with prejudice.
Distraught Tony Lee stared at the plates on the table, replete
with the usual trimmings, the holy instruments silverware, wood
and cloth. Victor Hitler, his daddy, a big daddy head cocked back
in a frown, and Mom, head down eyes closed as though already in
prayer. His little sister, the Shrew, sat staring blankly at nothing in
the distance.
Victor Hitler went now let us pray together.
He bowed his head and closed his eyes, folded his hands together, and Tony Lee saw the Shrew glancing at the faces of Mom
and Victor Hitler, such pious pieces of flesh.
Then she looked directly at him and silently mouthed her new
word of the day:
Asshole.
Tony Lee stared at her.
Mom looked askance at the Shrew and her little eyes snapped
down to her plate.
Victor Hitler cleared his throat
  intoning holiness thus—
    our father who art in heaven
      we thank you for this food
      and ask for your blessing
    and they all went amen
Knives cut then squeaking light scrapes across plates, forks
lifted and fell, clanking. Medium-rare pieces of meat bled brown-
ish fluids and clear yellow fat; Tony Lee saw the flash of a butter
knife blade, heard the distilled sound of people satiating their car-
nal needs, a wine glass tilted up and back down – then a soft burp
stifled by Victor Hitler.

—red face flushed, Tony Lee stared out the window of his room. Days had passed in lonely isolation, the power of a primary Victor Hitler interdiction. He was fantasizing about Christi, who he had not heard from again. But he couldn't get anywhere, because he was distracted by an argument he'd been having over the phone late nights with the Meat.

Dude, it's like, how old are you, anyway?

Tony Lee went eighteen.

The Meat went there ya go. You don't have to stay in your room. You know, I mean, Suzy has some friends that need a room-mate.

Jeez dude I can't just leave.

Why not?

Tony Lee didn't have an answer.

Staring at the outside, at the orderly streets of his neighborhood, he could see all the signs and omens of post-adolescent catastrophe: Chains and links of fencing and neatly trimmed hedges, manicured trees, precisely mown lawns, perfectly arranged vines drawn out, hooked and clipped together.

He saw none of that, but saw Christi's face, doing things he didn't think were allowed.

It built up, and Tony Lee went uhhhhh.

—the phone started ringing dull, turned low and covered with a pillow to prevent a loud ring. Tony Lee moved quick down the steps to answer.

Hello?

The Meat went hey Tony, get your ugly ass over to Roxanne's tomorrow.

Tony Lee went what for?

'Cause we're gonna jam out, that's what for.

Tony Lee went oh man, I can't.

Why the hell not?

Tony Lee was ashamed, but he admitted the pornographic truth: Because I'm still grounded.

Silence.

The Meat went like, I thought you were already eighteen.

Tony Lee went yeah, I am.

The Meat went dude, come on. Your parents can't ground you. You're a big boy now.

Tony Lee hesitated.

The Meat went well? Are you going to play guitar or not?

—down the alley Tony Lee pedaled, chains and gears a-whirr, past overflowing garbage cans, glittering smears of broken glass, a dead cat; a warm wind flapped his white T-shirt, the cuffs of jeans rolled up, black leather boots dirty and scuffed. His cheap guitar bag was slung over his back.

Smell of baking summer limestone, Tony Lee crossed a bridge over a dried out gully, stopped by a light at Lamar, shimmering summer heat, carbon monoxide wavelets burning up little flames. Then he pedaled hard, going uphill, long, past a fraternity house the boys in shorts and baseball caps assembling plywood World War II mock-ups, hateful party hearty, of which Victor Hitler dreamed, varsity College Life, the brotherhood of theme-party fraternity. Tony Lee sang out his answer: All I want is some action!

—Tony Lee arrived at Roxanne's place and let his bike fall in the dust; up the wooden porch Tony Lee clomped in his leather booted feet. His closed fist punched on the door and pretty soon it opened, holding the inside handle was a girl with purple hair and nose ring. Tony Lee knew it was Roxanne The Drummer.

She went hey, are you Tony Lee?

He went yeah that's me.

She went come on in.

It was dark inside and trash was strewn all over the floor. Piles of newspapers, hard-core porno mags, dirty clothes, empty cans and bottles, barbells and weights. On the couch sprawled the torso of a male manikin wearing crotchless panties and a push-up corset. Tony Lee's boots clomp-clomped following Roxanne through the living room into the kitchen. Junk and old food covered the counter tops. In one corner onions caked with dirt lay rotting. Dishes were piled in the sink unwashed and stained paper bags overflowed with trash.

A big dude with a shaved head stood under the harsh glow of a naked bulb stroking his fat fingers through a tub of margarine. He looked dully at Tony Lee and Roxanne while he smeared thick lumps of margarine into an aluminum cupcake tray.

He went hey.

Roxanne went Bald Peter this is Tony Lee.

Bald Peter nodded, saying nothing.

Behind him was a red plastic bowl filled with thick brown cupcake mix and a counter top mini-oven, the coils inside heating up, glowing red. Unknown black substances caked on the inside of the oven smoldered, emitting curly crisps of smoke that snaked into the air.

Roxanne went hey fool, don't burn 'em this time.

Bald Peter went hey, it ain't my fault they burned.

Roxanne went that's what happened to the last batch, Tony.

Tony Lee looked and saw six black charcoal briquettes lying on the floor next to a greasy trash sack.

Bald Peter's fingers stopped digging through the margarine.

He went hey, I was on the phone, okay?

Roxanne grabbed a beer from the fridge and pressed it into Tony Lee's hands and they went to the back room. Its yellowing walls were covered with all sorts of pornographic graffiti; moldy smelling mattresses sound-proofed the windows. It was a small room with a bare light bulb hanging from a cord. In the corner was Roxanne's simple drum set and there was a Fender mini-amp set up on a chair against the wall.

Roxanne went go ahead and plug in. I'll call the Meat and tell him to get his ass over here. He was all like, Tony Lee better be there on time. Then where the fuck is he? Nowhere.

Tony Lee flicked a cymbal with his finger.

Pash.

Then he opened his case and started plugging in. He wired his SG through a super distortion box, then turned on the amp, which crackled and sputtered furiously with the electronic blasts of failing guitar cord plugs.

Ping-pung of harmonic tuning.

Getting it right, Tony Lee went aah.

He slapped the open strings and took a big swig, guzzling down the Bud; he didn't like its mild metallic aftertaste but swigged it hard anyway – it was a frosty vaccination against Austin's brutal summertime heat.

—the shrill trill of feedback screech descended into a pattern from *AC/DC* heavy metal proto-punk power, *A Whole Lotta Rosie,* the first song Tony Lee had ever learned back when, now a thrash to warm up the fingers Tony Lee playing double time and Roxanne coming in on the drums and they hammered together and hammered the same thing for fifteen minutes till Tony's fret hand cramped up and Roxanne was panting out of breath.

When they stopped they heard the sharp peeping of the smoke detector, the clatter of aluminum and the panicked shrieks of Bald Peter. A moment later Bald Peter came in holding the aluminum cupcake form: Six charcoal briquettes.

Roxanne went oh man, you jerk.

Bald Peter went sorry.

He gave Tony Lee and Roxanne each a cold one to make up for ruining the cupcakes, then pried one the briquettes out with a butter knife and began munching on it, black crumbs tumbling to the floor.

They grossed out and Bald Peter went hey, I wouldn't eat 'em at all, but I ain't got nothin' else for dinner.

—they heard as the Meat came slamming through the front door shouting hey everybody, guess who's here.

He came to the back room and went that's right, it's me, the Meat.

He pointed with his finger at his chest.

The Meat went sorry I'm late, but I had to put an ad in the Chronicle for a bass player.

Roxanne went yeah?

Yeah, and it cost me seven bucks, so I need some money from you punks to cover the cost.

Roxanne went hey, we didn't ask you to do that.

The Meat went ah c'mon, it's only a couple bucks a piece.

Roxanne went all I can spare is two dollars. Gotta have some money for Raul's later.

Tony Lee went I got three bucks.

Bald Peter went hey, I got two bucks and that makes seven. Let's smoke out and then send Tony Lee to get beer.

Roxanne pulled a roach out of her T-shirt pocket and put it in her mouth. Bald Peter handed her a lighter and she snapped up a flame. Smoke curled and the tip glowed when she took a hit, her cheeks sucking in hard. She passed it to Bald Peter who took several tokes before the Meat hit him on the arm. By the time the Meat got the roach it was too small to hold without burning his fingers. He sucked on it, felt the sharp finger tip singe, sucked harder, and it flitted into his mouth.

—Tony Lee was on his bike going to Hyde Park Grocery. He ran a stop sign and tires screeched, a horn honked, and a big redneck leaned out of a pick-up truck stopped in the middle of the intersection.

He slapped his palm on the door and went hey, you stupid fucking *PUNK*.

Tony Lee pedaled faster and jumped a curb. In front of the store he let his bike fall to the cement and was in amongst the piles of fruit and vegetables. He looked at apples oranges pears mangoes. He picked up bananas and put them down, iceberg lettuce, broccoli and cauliflower.

Touching everything he then smelled his fingers.

A man stocking food gave him a hard stare; Tony Lee grinned, retreated to the beer display, and took some. The beer was cold, and riding furiously back to Roxanne's, Tony Lee, a twelve-pack of Bud under his arm.

Back at the house they did shotguns and played music. They shredded and hacked the songs they tried, a metallic fuzz without any bass, drums beating dry offbeat, screeching out of key the Meat. But the beer kept them wired till Roxanne unexpectedly passed out, falling and knocking over a cymbal stand. They carried her to bed, where she puked. They were all grossed out and felt sorry for her, but Tony Lee and the Meat refused to help Bald Peter clean up the mess. Instead they fought over the couch and Tony Lee won, the Meat lying down in the piles of trash on the floor, soon they were asleep.

—walking into Tony Lee's room, mom was disgusted. She found there clothes strewn on the floor, cassette tapes too, papers and books in piles. The carpet was filthy. She wondered why he never made the bed. At the same time she saw the dust covering all, even in the air: Floating motes of filth.

Downstairs Victor Hitler was cursing violently, she knew, an outrage that Tony had left the house while grounded. The bed, sign of her failure: Not made, not cared for, sheets in a tangled, dirty knot. She began to clean the room. She gathered armfuls of dirty clothes together and dumped them down a sheet metal chute; picked up books from the floor; shoes went into the closet, wadded bits of paper tossed. She picked up a pile of socks, wandered to the drawers, jerked one open.

Debris slid, her head nicked down, seeing a suspicious filth.

With a single dainty finger she poked through the stuff, removing in her time a partially smoked joint. Staring in wonder. Then, holding it between finger tips like it was some grotesque bug, mom backed out of the room.

—Roxanne was shaking Tony Lee's shoulder.

She went hey, get off the couch. We're going to Raul's.

Tony Lee went what?

He stumbled into the bathroom and looked at his face which was stamped with couch fabric pattern. He blinked his eyes and saw that some hairs on his lower cheek stuck out. Opening the mirror, he found a plastic disposable shaver, and began sliding it around his face and chin.

As he worked Bald Peter came in to take a leak.

Bald Peter went hey, don't use that razor.

Tony Lee went why not?

Because that's the one I use to shave my pubes.

—leaving the house in a hurry, they got to Guadalupe Street in time to catch a bus. Each paid a quarter to the slot, rocked and lurched down the aisle heading for the empty seats at the back, passengers eying them suspiciously. At the back they sat down, laughing, ribbing each other, laughing more; Tony Lee cast an accidental glance out the window and saw a man furtively going into Relaxation Plus massage – parlor of masturbation stare – but his short laugh quickly turned to astonishment: The man he'd seen was Victor Hitler.

Tony Lee went hey, bodies in action!

They went what?

Jumping up, jaw jutting down, he went to his friends hey, I just saw Victor Hitler going into the massage parlor.

The Meat went naw, really?

They all craned to look back but the bus was too far, they saw nothing; a few blocks down they pushed a button and climbed out.

Roxanne went hey, who's playin'?

Bald Peter went the *Dicks*.

The Meat went hey, I know the singer Gary, I partied once with Gary.

At the door a brute in chains was taking money. His skin head glistened with oils.

He went three bucks each.

They paid up and went inside. All the tables were pushed back towards the wall to make space for the crowd and for the slam dancing. A guy on stage plugged monitors in and messed with microphones, adjusted electro-boxes, taped cords down. The Meat got a pitcher at the bar, they drank from plastic cups, the crowd growing, Tony Lee saw good punk cuts and clothes. He gazed through the crowd and over by the bar he saw a hot girl, a platinum blond. Tony Lee tugged on the Meat's T-shirt.

He went hey Meat, isn't that Christi?

The Meat went yeah man, that's Christi. Suzy Creamcheese told me Christi wants you.

Tony Lee took a drink and went all right.

They finished off the pitcher and the Meat bought another one. Bald Peter and Roxanne were together, Bald Peter had his hands on her butt. He was supersized and she was so very tiny, Tony Lee couldn't imagine them having sex unless she did the top. They acted like they'd known each other their whole lives. It must be love, thought Tony Lee.

The Meat went hey, if I were you I'd go over and say hi to Christi. Suzy said basically all you'd have to do is ask.

Tony Lee went all right.

He made his way through the crowd to Christi.

He went hey, Christi.

She went hey, Tony. I didn't know you liked the *Dicks*.

He went I never heard of them.

Christi went I heard they're recording this show tonight. Maybe if we shout loud enough we'll be famous.

Tony Lee went I guess so.

She went well Tony, what have you been doing?

I've been playing guitar.

Are you in a band?

Me and the Meat are startin' one. Original punk only. He writes the songs and sings. I play guitar. Roxanne plays drums. All we need is a bass player.

What's the name of it?

Tony Lee went well the Meat said *The Slash*, but I said that sucks. And then Roxanne came up with *meatpiston*.

Christi's eyes got big and she went *meatpiston*?

Then she lauged.

Are you any good?

No.

Christi laughed again and went hey all right. Wanna beer?

—just then the crowd surged forward and the lights dimmed.

The *Dicks* were getting on stage.

Shouts came from the crowd and Christi and Tony Lee pushed into the throng. She was right in front of him hopping up and down on her tip toes and sticking her ass out it rubbed against Tony Lee. He felt people behind him and pushed forward. She stopped hopping and stood on her toes stretching her head up to see, her ass sticking out pushing harder against Tony Lee's swelling crotch. Every time Christi moved he felt it get bigger, and she kept moving.

Gary the singer was on stage with his back to the crowd. He said something to the other guys in the band and shook his head.

Someone yelled hey, fuck the police

Gary spun around, grabbed the microphone. He screwed up his face and went ah don't say that they're new wave

And *The Police* were New Wave. Why would anyone hate on that anyway? But in that instant the *Dicks* busted into *Fake Bands* and the crowd was hopping with the guitar thrash a spring popping up down so fast the beer spills out the cup and Tony Lee saw the

Meat up front at the stage starting to slam and he grabbed Christi's waist and felt her taut body and he liked it; Christi felt Tony Lee's hands on her hips and felt him pressing against her. She felt his bulge and it turned her on and as soon as the show was done she wanted to leave and fuck and fuck fuck fuck. Up front there was a wild swishing back and forth as the Meat succeeded in breaking into full thrash slam a wave pushing back and forth and arms busting faces punching guts.

They played hard and the crowd bounced and sweated and then the song was over. Christi had the panicked blood, the hormone reaction heat to fuck, she turned around and grabbed the back of Tony Lee's head, pulled his face down and kissed. They kissed, and her tongue was where he wanted it in his mouth and they heard Gary yell at someone in the audience he went take a lesson, asshole

And Tony Lee slid his hand down, squeezing in the depths of the crowd, hidden, her puss from in front, her skirt jacked-up by his forearm in the dark. Screams and shouts from the crowd and a moment of electronic hum then the guitar intoned, and it was all about *Dicks Hate Police.*

The slamming had stopped up front and the crowd was close in on each other breathing like a single animal slopping down beers and stomping leather booted foot on filth smeared cement floor.

—after the set Christi went hey I've got some crank at my house you want some?

Tony Lee went I just want to go to your house.

They struggled through the thick crowd and over by the window Tony Lee saw the Meat kissing Suzy Creamcheese. Tony Lee followed Christi out of the club onto the street. He looked at her legs that flashed white below her black leather mini-skirt. She looked back and saw him looking at her, felt the surge again, went you know, the first time I saw you at Suzy's party I thought to myself man, I want to get laid by that guy.

Tony Lee went that's all I'm thinking about right now.

Then they were at her car, little Toyota hum, and driving down Guadalupe him watching her legs work the pedals in the flash of nighttime dim light glassed-in box. She ground the gears shifting up after turning west on 24th, the hem of her skirt moving up so that he could see the top of her thighs, could see the tendon working her knee joint.

She watched him watching and went you wanna see more, don't you Tony?

Tony Lee went yes.

A few miles later, after dips and sway, just before MoPac express, she turned right and they drove perhaps another minute before she pulled up an inclined driveway, turned off the motor at the top. They got out, did not touch each other's flesh, then inside the house.

Christi went hey Tony, wanna beer?

Sure.

They split the only beer in the fridge.

Christi went come on upstairs to my room.

He followed her up the stairs, which opened into a high ceilinged room, painted dirty off-white, windows all around. There was a delicate wooden bed with canopy and matching rocking chair painted both glossy white. She had postered the walls with punk band pictures from magazines, record stores, an oval white rug on the floor.

He went wow, where'd you get this stuff?

She went the bed and chair were my grandma's.

Tony Lee sat down in the rocking chair and took a gulp from the beer. He rocked back and forth. Christi sat across from him on the bed.

She went this is a cool house, it's only $250 a month.

He went that's a lot.

She went I'm working part time at a jewelry store.

Then they sat for a moment staring at each other and he looked at her legs. She moved the right one in and out. The mini skirt lifted and fell, lifted and fell.

She went I like to tease the frat boys in my finance class. I sit in back of them wearing this skirt and start talking to them and when they turn around they can see my panties.

He went they can? What do they do about it?

They don't do nothin'.

Tony Lee went I wouldn't do nothin'.

Tony Lee was rocking in the chair and she sat across from

him and he looked straight between her slightly opened thighs. She saw him looking there and it stamped her blood. It was quiet in the room. Then she leaned back on the bed, supporting her weight on her elbows, leaning back so her shirt rested on her flat stomach and her breasts pointed up, cupped by the red of the shirt, and the white legs on tiptoe slightly parted. The thighs crept farther apart and the skirt pulled up and Tony Lee could see more.

Then Christi went so why don't you fuck me, Tony Lee?

—it had been a kind of clumsy fuck and had ended way too soon but it made them only hotter for each other. They lay bodies dark on the white bed linen. Tony Lee with his eyes closed and she stroked her hand up and down his leg and torso. Christi liked his big thighs.

She touched them more and it started turning her on and so she went c'mon Tony, let's fuck again.

She grabbed his wank and it stood up under her kneading but a rattling car pulled up to the house with music blaring and Christi stopped moving.

She went oh hell, I think it's Chuck.

Tony Lee went who's Chuck?

Christi looked at him her dark brows raised in shrug.

She went my ex-boyfriend.

Down below Chuck got out of his broken-up VW and yelled.

He went hey Christi I know you're in there.

Christi put on a nightie kind of see-through shirt from her dresser top and went to the open window. Tony Lee looked at her from behind, an outline of her body through the material; saw the bottom curve of her butt below the hem, thin legs slendering to the floor, nervous pulling and bunching of the nightie in clenching fists.

Chuck went hey Christi.

She went oh man what do you want?

I want you.

Christi went ah Chuck, get the fuck out of here. We broke up and that's all.

The shaven head of Chuck rocked back and forth on its hinges, he opened his hands wide.

Oh man Christi, like, why are you being so mean to me?

Chuck, just go away. I don't want to talk to you.

Why not?

'Cause I'm trying to sleep.

But I just want to ask you some questions.

Just leave, dude. It's over.

No I don't want to leave.

You get the hell out of here or I'll call the cops.

Crimson flushed the face of Chuck and his middle finger unrolled from his fist and fucked the air rapidly, driven by the angry thrusts of his skinny, T-shirted arm.

The two antagonists gazed hotly at the face of their ex-other.

Man, right now I hate you, Christi.

Christi went I hope it tastes good.

Then she slammed the window shut on Chuck.

Lying on the bed with fast beating heart Tony Lee heard a curse of anger and then the door of a car clatter; the sound of a VW engine rattled into function. As the car drove off Tony Lee slipped up behind Christi, who felt a hardon press against her butt. She reached down and grabbed it. Tony Lee rested his neck lightly for a moment on her shoulder crook, then grunted as she took him in, pumping framed by the window, a moving painting on the outside wall, Jugendstil dark sin fuck until thick splatter of moaned up love, seen from outside across the street through the high-powered telescope of a frantically masturbating Peeping Tom.

—standing on his front lawn, Tony Lee watched the taillights of Christi's car recede, brighten for a moment at an intersection, then disappear around a corner. Key struggled with lock, not finding hole, then inside the clock on the wall showing three-thirty. He stood at the entrance to the living room, swaying, holding onto the jamb, ears still ringing from the punk show. He saw mom passed out on the couch, a half full glass of whisky on a nearby table and an empty bottle of Jack Daniels lying on the Persian-carpeted floor. He went over and his face peered into hers, listened to her deep breathing, twitching nostrils smelling the rank alcohol fuzz. She snored lightly. When he reached up and snapped off the lamp she moaned and turned over. Victor Hitler was still out, Tony Lee knew where, bodies in action, he yawned and dragged himself upstairs to bed.

—a firm knock.

Tony Lee turned in his bed, a beer hangover disturbing his belly and brain, the gas in his intestines.

Once again came the fist on wood: Clop-clop.

Tony Lee went oh man, what?

The door opened, a crack of light jabbed into Tony Lee's conscious like a steel wedge.

Victor Hitler stalked stiff to the window reflection of light reflected through prism; pain cracking open his sleep, muttering—

Victor Hitler went good God, the stench.

Jerking open the shutters, ka-whap ka-whap ka-whap jerking open the window, skra-lee-skra-lee-thunk.

Tony Lee put his head under the pillow.

Victor Hitler leaned out breathing in the fresh air. Then he turned around. On the sill, sitting with hands turned in on knees, arms akimbo. He stared at the motionless form under the covers on the bed. He shook his head, sensation between despair and disappointment and anger. Suspicions no longer, but fact: Tony Lee was smoking marijuana.

Tony Lee stirred, pulled the cover from his head, deformed hair stiff sticking out.

The shame, thought Victor Hitler, and Tony Lee squinting and rubbing his face.

Tony Lee went what time is it?

Victor Hitler went time for you to get up and come downstairs. Your mother and I want to talk to you.

But it's so early.

Get up and come downstairs.

Tony Lee looked at Victor Hitler.

He went I didn't do nothin' wrong.

Victor Hitler walked to the door and went hurry up.

Tony Lee got up and went to the bathroom, relieved his hard bloated bladder. He splashed water in his face, brushed his teeth. The hangover cracked the veins in his brain and his underarms stank.

Tony Lee sniffed them, grimaced, and went ooh.

Then he got dressed: Torn jeans, a T-shirt, laced up black high-top boots from Goodwill. For extra effect, in what he figured would be some kind of good old-fashioned bitching-out, he put on his black belt with metal studs that Suzy Creamcheese had given him at the party. Then he went down to the living room.

—mom sat on the couch and Victor Hitler on one of the dining table chairs; they were looking at Tony Lee gravely as he walked into the living room.

Tony Lee sat down on the armchair across from them.

He went so, what's the matter?

Victor Hitler frowned.

It's about your future.

Tony Lee made an odd face, like pink tongue pushing out; he slumped back in the chair, booted feet splayed, arms limp on the fat upholstery.

Victor Hitler went hey, this is serious.

Tony Lee went okay.

Victor Hitler went these last few months you've been acting weird, you've been staying out later and later and then, suddenly, you come home wearing outrageous clothes and you have this, this crazy haircut.

Tony Lee went there's nothing wrong with my haircut.

Victor Hitler went not every personal choice is okay.

Tony Lee groaned inwardly, kept face straight staring at his boots.

He went what are you talking about? I didn't do anything wrong.

Victor Hitler reached over to the table, took something from it. Daintily, he held it up for inspection.

Maybe you can tell us what you're doing with this?

When Tony Lee saw the joint he knew that he was fucked.

He went hey, that's not mine.

Don't start lying Tony Lee. You're mother found it in one of your drawers.

Tony Lee went that's not mine that belongs to somebody else.

Victor Hitler went I don't care who it belongs to. What mat-

30

ters is that you're in possession of an illegal *drug*.

Tony Lee said nothing.

Victor Hitler put the joint back down.

He went so, your mother and I have decided that it would be in your best interest for you to attend a four week program at the Faulkner Home.

Tony Lee's head snapped up.

Incredulous, he grinned and went what?

Eyes examined eyes.

Victor Hitler went that's right. We're sending you to the Faulkner Home for drug rehab.

Tony Lee went you gotta be kidding.

Mom went I don't want my son to be a junkie.

Tony Lee went this is ridiculous I'm not a junkie.

Then what are you doing with a dangerous drug? Who'd you get it from?

Tony Lee went good God, it's just half a joint. I don't do drugs. I drink beer. But I don't need the Faulkner Home for that, do I?

From now you're not to have any contact with this character, what do you call him, the Meat? For God's sake what the hell kind of person is named *the Meat*?

Mom looked at Victor Hitler.

She went honey, you promised to keep your temper.

Victor Hitler waved her away.

He went well? What kind of a person is this *Meat*?

Tony Lee went it's just a nickname his real name is Marty.

No more Marty. He isn't your friend. And none of his wacko buddies are either.

Tony Lee clenched and rapidly unclenched muscle.

He went you can't tell me who I can have as friends.

This Monday we're checking you into the Faulkner Home for drug rehabilitation and that's the final word. Until then you're not to leave the house—

You're crazy, man.

Victor Hitler stood and pointed.

He went I'm not crazy, you're the one that's crazy.

Mom went honey!

Tony Lee went man, I'm fucking sick of this shit. You're like some kind of god damned Nazi, that's what you are.

Victor Hitler went don't you curse in my house.

Tony Lee went you're more worried about me saying 'god damned' than you are about being a Nazi. What an asshole.

Victor Hitler, stiff body going to spring—

Tony Lee went I say fuck this shit.

Victor Hitler moved quickly forward and Tony Lee jumped up from the chair. Victor Hitler took a swing but Tony Lee ducked.

Mom screamed *no!*

Victor Hitler tried to make another go of it, but Tony Lee swung first hitting his dad solid in the gut.

Hooooh!

Victor Hitler stumbled back clutching his belly.

Mom screamed again and went you hit your father you hit your father.

She marched straight over to Tony Lee and stood directly in front of him, tears wet in her eyes, and with a sudden wild swipe scratched the shit out of Tony Lee's face who ran screaming—

    you both gone crazy

      you both gone crazy

        and Tony Lee stinging pain

         fingernail-bloodied cheek

         bashing out the door

         huffing radical down the street

—days later the Meat and Tony Lee clomped up the wooden steps of a porch in their scruffy leather boots. The Meat clapped his fist on a flimsy screen door. No one answered.

The Meat went hey Butthole, hey Veronica.

Then he hit the screen door harder and yelled again.

Through a brown dusted window pane peeped the Meat, saw no one. He knocked again, no answer. He turned the knob. The door opened a crack, jammed on the floor. The Meat huffed and grunted and shoved. The door rattled open revealing deeply grooved scratches on stained hardwood.

The Meat's face brightened at Tony Lee.

He went hey man, it's unlocked.

Together, they entered the dark house. Wall paper hung down

in great torn sheets, paint peeled from the ceiling, heaps of garbage trash and dust balls careened in the wake of their slow passage through the wreckage. They saw a broken chair with only three legs. It stood crooked, the forth leg replaced by a dented toaster. They saw a fifty-gallon plastic garbage can overflowing with trash like a gigantic scoop of ice cream. The bare studs of one wall divided the living room from the TV room – no drywall.

They walked through the house inspecting, and while the Meat continued down the hallway Tony Lee paused and flicked on the light in the bathroom – roaches scattered.

The Meat re-appeared at the bathroom door and laughed.

He went hey, they were in the back room doin' it. They said you could have the spare room.

The Meat kicked open the door across from the bathroom. It was an extra large closet with no windows. There was a strong musty smell and a bare overhead light. Wide shelves ran along the two opposing walls, on poles underneath a few wire clothes hangers.

Tony Lee nodded and went hey, this is all right.

—waiting until Victor Hitler was at work and Mom and the Shrew had gone shopping they sneaked in through the backyard mid-afternoon and went up the back outside stairway. It creaked and groaned and scared them a little.

Tony Lee hurried and went we gotta be fast, man.

The Meat went just do it.

They opened the balconey back door, which Tony Lee knew would be unlocked, and they dashed through the hallway to his old room and they grabbed the mattress off Tony Lee's bed. They struggled with the twin, bustling down the hallway and then to the wooden outside stairs again and struggled to bend the mattress around the tight landing halfway down.

Tony Lee went god dammit don't shove motherfucker don't shove.

The Meat went I'm not shovin' hurry up god dammit shit I'm about to drop it—

The fingers of the Meat let loose and the sudden weight transfer made Tony Lee tumble.

Down he went, bowled over by the mattress for the last of the steps, cursing as he fell, landing all heaped up at the bottom with the mattress flopping on top.

The Meat cackled.

Tony Lee went god dammit Meat, you're supposed to be the strong one.

They picked it up again and slid it across the grass and the yard, the two boys charging with the bending, flopping mattress.

The Meat went hurry up hurry up hurry up.

Going through the gait the mattress sagged sideways, caught on a wire, and was ripped open.

Tony Lee went ah man, fuck. Fuck!

Then they were on their bicycles fighting the mattress and huffing and the Meat's front tire crashing again and again into the back wheel of Tony Lee. They ran stop signs and kept to side streets scared of the cops. At an intersection the Meat misjudged and crashed them into a curb. They fell, both dropping the mattress and spilling out onto the grass.

Tony Lee jumped up and went god dammit Meat, what the fuck are you doin'?

The Meat saw him and roared laughing at the sky.

Pointing, he shouted like man, look at your shirt.

The head of Tony Lee nicked down, hands snapping T-shirt taut, and he saw the broad smear on his chest of yellow-brown dogshit turd.

—a house defiled.

Surveying Tony Lee's deserted room Victor Hitler went hell honey I hate to think we've raised such an irresponsible ass.

The eyes of mom were open wide, they traced the outlines of the mattress-less bed frame. One thin finger on her chin, she shook her head.

Mom went I don't get it.

Where the hell is he? asked Victor Hitler, in agony barely concealed.

Mom went well, at least this means he's not sleeping in the bushes.

Victor Hitler grunted.

He went well, you never know.

—at a table Tony Lee worked on the application, and finishing it he gave it to the cashier.

She went okay, I'll give it to the manager.

Tony Lee went outside, bright sun a-simmering; big Bald Peter was sitting on a big landscape boulder, sweat glistening on his skin; he looked suddenly up.

So?

Tony Lee went so.

Bald Peter went like, just get on god damned welfare. Once a week you have to turn in a list of three companies you've applied to. Make sure and apply for positions you're not qualified for, then you'll never be hired.

But Tony Lee went hey, I wanna work.

Bald Peter made a face and shook his head.

He went you're a moh-ron. You can make more money on welfare or selling weed. That's what Eddie does. He's got a whole god damned trashcan full of it at his trailer.

—darkness and sprinkles of metal on metal. On his back in the tiny windowless room, Tony Lee listened to the tingle of clothes hangers he occasionally bumped with a stick. Fruits of independence, what he was after, not to be bumming away.

Thoughts of the proper life, and Christi breathing soft nearby, she snored in a cute way, Tony Lee butted her lightly, his elbow jabbing a rib.

She went hey, why'd 'ya do that?

You was snorin'.

For a few moments there was silence, broken then by the footfall of Butthole who entered the bathroom across, the sound of his piss splattering loudly the toilet water and rim.

Christi went hey, don't you think this room is a little depressing? What kind of a god damned life do you wanna lead, anyway? I mean, wouldn't you rather have a real room in a proper house?

Tony Lee went hey, what are ya, Victor Hitler? All he talks about is proper this, proper that. He says there's a right way to live and a wrong way to live. Hell, all I care about is action, more action – and even more action.

Christi giggled.

Well there ain't much room for action in here, buster.

What? Are you makin' fun of my castle?

Castle?

Sure, ain't you ever heard, a man's home is his castle?

Across the hall, Butthole finished up and flushed the toilet, burped obnoxiously, and wandered off leaving toilet water gurgles, mechanical squeaks and moans.

—the manager of the Omelettry West restaurant called Tony Lee on the phone, told him to report the next morning to work.

The first day he learned the cookery of omelettes and hot cakes, then TexMex, spatula turning steam up and pouring out mixture for more. Hot in the kitchen, they had big fans running blowing the hot fresh air from outside into the hot smoky air of the kitchen. Reuben was the head cook, big fat dude, sweating, face glistening brown sheen. Tony Lee was pretty sure Reuben didn't like him.

When he could Reuben went back to the office and took hits from a flat man bottle of whisky. On the third day, Reuben called Tony Lee into the office and closed the door.

He went hey man, you want to take a shot?

Surprised, Tony Lee went sure.

Reuben took a shot from his bottle, gave it to Tony Lee, but when he lifted the bottle and tilted his head back, lips pursing to slam the whiskey down, Reuben suddenly opened the door. Just outside was the owner, talking, but he turned and saw Tony Lee, throat mid-bob, swallowing the firewater.

—at Christi's Tony Lee arched his back. All of tension muscle bunches, fluid swelling in functioning glandwork, streaming upward in the dreamy bob of head. Various smells of Christi had floated up to him, her hands across his naked chest and belly, him touching the blond platinum of her hair.

Her neck muscles tensed and released, tensed and released.

It was a pulling of fluid, and she looked briefly into his eyes, his hardened stem poking at luscious creamy softness.

Christi unplugged it and worked it slow with her hand.

She went you're about to come, aren't you?

Tony Lee shuddered, pushed up.

Fast she bobbed and it seemed as though the rush began from the farthest

 and gazing alternately

  between the canopy white netting and the posts

   hearing always the bed spring creak creak

  and the platinum blonde hair

   his brown hands as stars clutching round the curved

  surface of her skull the pretty head bobbing

  the tight slurp of encircling lip a little tighter

  the bed spring creaking

   her lips tighter—

    and Tony Lee went uuuuuuhhh

—the foreman at the print shop, Alvarez, smiled a druggy smile Tony Lee would never trust. Long skinny arms, tattooed, pointed out this and that; Tony Lee nodded his head, distracted however by the shiny machineries that revolved, jutted, and clattered; distracted by the tattoos. He puzzled and finally deciphered the faded blue flowery lettering on stringy biceps—

"fuck gringo"

Alvarez ended the tour at the end of a long seven-color print machine, smiled again at Tony Lee. They stood before a rack, it was the sheet feeder device, of which Tony Lee was to supply with large sheets of heavy poster paper. It came in big bundles, two and a half by three feet, each bundle weighing 63 pounds. Skinny little Alvarez grabbed a bundle, slapped it down in the feeder column.

He went whatever you do, don't let the feeder column run out of paper. It fucks things up.

Tony Lee went okay.

Alvarez walked down the line, stopped at a control board. He smiled back at Tony Lee.

He went ready?

Tony Lee went sure.

Alvarez grabbed a lever, pushed, the lever moved, and machinery began spinning.

Paper was sucked from the feeder at an alarming rate.

Alvarez laughed and shouted: Go, man, go!

Every minute or so the machine needed another bundle; when Tony Lee was running out of bundles Alvarez brought a forklift with a new pallet-full, and working continuously, the pallet was emptied out about once an hour.

During break Alvarez came up to Tony Lee, who slumped exhausted on a stool by the feeder.

He went hey, why you wanna work in the print shop?

Tony Lee went like, I read you could make 20 bucks an hour.

Alvarez made face at Tony Lee.

He went man, you believe that? How much you makin' now?

Three fifty.

Alvarez laughed hard.

He went I been here ten years I'm makin' 12 bucks an hour.

Alvarez walked away. Tattoed on his shoulder blade were a purple snake and skull, and the backside of his faded and tattered bell-bottomed jeans were brown, sagging flat.

—behind giggling Christi crept Tony Lee, underbrush and twigs crackling under footfall's step: They were at the Woodshock Punkfest, in progress, booming out over the dry limestone bedrock cracking dried scrub oak wood, splitting eardrum, fading then in far away distances to a dumb, muted silence.

In the woods they pinched and grabbed various portions of each other's flesh, pausing at one point in the dark by a broken tree to kiss, hearing the voices of nearby pandemonium. Their tongues tasted of whiskey and beer, the faint stink of near alcohol saturation, dulled by the buzz.

Tony Lee went how long between sets?

Golly I don't know, but I sure am hungry.

A cackling laugh boomed out through the woods, general screams ensued; they heard a breaking bottle shatter into silent shards, absorbed for the next eon by forest floor humus. In the distance, holding hands, Tony Lee and Christi were giggling, which turned to cursing when they stumbled through an unpleasant surprise of wicked thorn bush. But once they tore through that, with scratched arms and growling stomachs, they walked down the asphalt road to The Salt Lick.

Tony Lee went it's right up there, see it?

The smells of meat and hickory smoke drifted, a car full of punks blaring music careened by, someone tossed a firecracker. It fizzled at Christi's feet and exploded – strobing them

shock Egyptian dance

Soon they were seated in the Salt Lick barbecue heaven.

It was near capacity with screaming obnoxious punks taking refuge in delicacies brought in great heaping piles to their tables, pig meat double-bowl chicken-feed cow-flesh fuck, an orgy of sizzling oils, fats, and charbroiled blood. They found a table and ordered family plates; in long streams of sinewed flesh they fed themselves satiating unrepressed hunger, Christi laughing as Tony Lee fed her brisket, flicking pieces briefly with tongue, her face smeared with sauce, bright eyes beaming, and slopping down viciously beer.

—the print shop job was four days a week and Tony Lee started coming in drunk. He sang to himself while feeding the machine its heavy bundles of paper. He shouted and laughed, the operators grinned, Alvarez grinned, for they had all started there, at the feeder column. Tony Lee slept under the seven color Heidelberg press during the half hour break, it smelling of ink and cleaning solution and oil, sleep then, until the bell sounded and the insane rhythmic hammering woke him.

Once he let the feeder column run out of paper, and the machine shut down. Alvarez came running over, furious, roaring, frothing.

He went *hey, you stupid FUCK.*

Then he grabbed a fresh bundle of paper from the pallet and threw it onto the ground. The paper scattered in every direction. Alvarez pointed at it.

Now, you pick that shit up.

Tony Lee went hey, all right.

Half an hour later, machinery spinning again, Alvarez came up grinning, sweating, stinking.

He went hey man, like, next time it happens, you're fired.

—another night at Raul's.

Christi was cranked out running everywhere talking to someone for a moment then moving to someone else. The Meat was talking with some skinny dude with a purple Afro and Tony Lee drank his beer at a table with Butthole and Veronica who were arguing about something stupid. Tony Lee finished his beer and went to the Meat.

The Meat went hey Tony, this is Sammy-san.

Tony Lee and Sammy-san each went hey.

Casual meeting, they bumped shoulders.

The Meat went hey Tony, Sammy-san plays bass.

Tony Lee went yeah?

Sammy-san went yeah.

The Meat went we're gonna jam tomorrow and Sammy-san's gonna bring his PA.

Tony Lee went hey!

The Meat ordered beer and they all slammed it down. Tony Lee went like, what kind of PA is it?

Sammy-san went it's a Carvin with sixteen channels.

Tony Lee went all right, like, I gotta tell Christi about it. He looked for Christi and found her by the door; she was standing real cool and talking to Chuck. He said something and Christi laughed, then she stretched up and gave him a kiss on the cheek. Tony Lee returned to the bar, drank more beer with the Meat and Sammy-san, suds it down, the foam on the top of the beer in the cups that tastes so bitter. Later Tony Lee looked and saw that Christi and Chuck were gone, slammed his remaining brew in one slug.

He went Meat, pour me another.

They listened to the *Sex Pistols* on the house stereo and downed two pitchers. People they knew came by and asked about their band, talked about parties, about the scene, about maybe going to New York or LA, maybe even London, sitting at the bar getting drunker, waiting for something to happen, but nothing happened.

The Meat went man, what kind of Saturday night is this? It's a fucking bore in here.

40

Sammy-san went hey: All I want is some action!

Down with the beers, and watching through the crowd Tony Lee saw flighty stumbling little Christi come back in, laughing, grabbing, falling against the wall, legs giving way sliding straight for the floor where Bruno the Doorman would have to scoop her up and remove her via the bum's rush face-first plunge: Through the front door to the sidewalk outside. Off the stool Tony Lee bounded, pushing past tight bodies to the wall in time to prop her up, twist her head up, the lolling eyes that refused to focus on him.

She was nodding.

Tony Lee went hey, hey Christi what you been doin'?

The half-closed eyes rested for a moment on his face, the warmth of her underarms where his hands crutched her up, a blitz of recognition at least, and a smile.

She went ah Tony, it's you.

And her arms up around his neck and the head lolled free, falling forward against him, blacked out. Tony Lee held her pinned tight on the wall, keeping her from collapsing.

He went hey Christi, come on, snap out of it. You've had way too much. What'd you do with Chuck? What did you take?

Christi went Tony, I gotta get to the bathroom.

And again her head seemed to loll, but then she came alive, all tight muscle struggling to get away and Tony Lee who tried to hold her until she suddenly hissed, jerking her arms away and she went, hey, hey, let me go. I'm not a fucking baby.

Tony Lee released her and she lurched forward into a crowd and went look out, I'm gonna be sick! She puked then into the mass of standing bodies that rapidly split open with curses and shoves, Christi fell on the floor.

Tony Lee went ahh shit.

Bruno the Doorman was charging and Tony Lee picked up limp Christi who was muttering oh man oh man I'm sorry and with her slowly working her legs assisting him they made it outside under the stern supervision of Bruno the Doorman. Tony Lee took her to the parking lot where they spoke.

Damn, what are you on?

I just had a rush.

What'd ya take?

A quaalude.

Oh man, Christi, you shouldn't be mixing 'ludes and crank and alcohol, it's too much.

Christi pulled away from Tony Lee and went man, I'm all right.

Tony Lee went hey, if it wasn't for me the doorman would've busted your ass.

Ahh, fuck that shit.

And hey, what about Chuck, anyway?

Christi went nuthin'.

Tony Lee went I saw you kissin' that fucker.

Christi's head twisted up following her eyes that traced the path of the moon through the heavens – but it was a moonless night.

She went well Chuck's been a lot nicer than you're being.

A while back you never wanted to see him again.

I'll see him anytime I want.

Tony Lee turned around and went what the fuck.

He started walking back to the club, but then he turned and pointed at her under the parking lot lights with his finger.

He went hey Christi, you still got puke on your face.

Christi muttered incoherently some curses and fumbled in her purse for the keys to her car, trying vaguely to remember ... to remember ... she was leaving, right? And where the fuck had she parked and did she even have the fucking keys to her car? All she could find in her little purse was a make-up mirror, which she opened to see if Tony was lying about the puke.

—inside Raul's Tony Lee found the Meat and Sammy-san. They bought another pitcher and got three fresh plastic cups. They began slamming down Buds and Tony Lee felt all right, he really did, and they waited for Butthole, who came by after the world had disintegrated into obliquely associated parts, whose mouth went hey, the party's on for tonight. The Meat, talking with Suzy Cream-cheese. The new tiger-stripe haired Roxanne and Bald Peter.

The Meat went hey, let's go.

Tony Lee saw Butthole and Veronica going out the door with Suzy Creamcheese. The Meat was talking to a bunch of girls near the door then they were out on the street and like in a high wind where Tony Lee couldn't hear.

The Meat went over at the house and drive?

Tony Lee went what?

It was like wind in his ears and then after that a blur of lights and suddenly they were at the house inside and the stereo blasted a *Black Flag TV Party* bash and Butthole shouted and the people jamming out to the hilarious tune and they had beer and stood on the porch and suddenly Sammy-san came out of the house with a board.

He came up to the Meat and went hey man, hold this for me just like this.

Then Sammy-san held the board in front of himself, arms outstretched, one hand on the top and one hand on the bottom. The Meat nodded and took it from him and held it.

He went like this?

Sammy-san went yeah, just like that. Hold it tight as hell.

Then Sammy-san sort of crouched like a kung-fu dude, and then he freaked everyone out because he started shouting fuck you bitch fuck you bitch fuck you!

Then screaming he executed a perfect high-side kick right in the middle of the board, which snapped suddenly in two.

The crowd went wow.

Sammy-san looked at the Meat and went yeah that's where the "san" comes from man. 'Cause that's what they called me in my Kung-fu class up in Killeen.

The keg was in the back and they all went in and filled up a cup and talked music. Sammy-san was gung-ho and wanted to play real bad. He liked how the Meat's songs sounded.

He went I can play that shit. That shit will be awesome shit and we are going to play the shit out of that shit.

Tony Lee went yeah!

He had gotten so drunk that the wider party began to disappear from what he perceived. Everything was right now and only right now. What was in front of him and what was behind him – that no longer existed.

Later some hippie wandered in and gave out blotter acid talking about free love and peace, man, and Tony Lee was so wasted he took it and the Meat and everyone took it. Nothing happened for a while and then they started to hallucinate *Black Flag* on acid and they just knew they were going to rise above the nonsensical Victor Hitler bullshit.

The hippie went let's go for a drive.

Sammy-san went you're fuckin' crazy man.

City lights flashing, scream out the window at a transient on Guadalupe Street. The hippie was at the wheel and then on Barton Springs road and bouncing over a curb at Zilker Park spinning around without lights on the soccer fields roaring past the rock outcrop losing control somewhere near the MoPac bridge. The car got stuck axle deep in the mud and the hippie staggered off in the dark crying.

They deserted him.

Walking in the buzzing fluorescence they crossed over the pedestrian river bridge. The lights made all their skin look different colors than they normally looked, especially different looking on acid. Tony Lee thought his skin looked greenish-blue and showed everyone.

The Meat went *I knew it!*

Tony Lee went what?

I always knew you were an alien.

Sammy-san looked around and went wow, now nobody's white.

Everyone laughed.

Then they were over the bridge in the dark heading down Lake Austin boulevard, because Butthole wanted to go to the golf course and run in the sprinklers naked.

He went it's the freakiest shit on acid.

There were almost no cars driving down the street.

The Meat went man all this quiet is freaking me out.

But when they were almost to the golf coarse they started hearing a weird sound, kind of like the sound of crashing metal, and at the same time thundering bass and twang.

Butthole stopped and went hey, what the fuck is that?

The Meat went I don't know, but it's freaking me out even more than the quiet.

They stood in the middle of the street wondering, and the sound got closer and louder and louder.

Suddenly a fat ball of red sparks exploded around the street corner one block up, coming straight at them—

The Meat screamed *OH FUCK RUN!*
    and feet stomping pavement they ran
      hearts beating wild in their chests panic exploding
   in their heads
  and arms and feet
the ball of sparks and fire clattering straight at them until
crying out they dived onto a nearby lawn, tumbled and lay flat or
crouched – ready to run again – and watched wide-eyed as a pick-
up truck blaring country and western music without its lights on
dieseled past towing a clattering, bouncing, metal garbage can on
a chain.

Then, like all things on acid – it was gone.

—back at the house they found somebody lying in the front
yard puking, and they just stood there looking at him. Later on they
rode bicycles to the Meat's to get more beer and the Meat smashed
head-on into a parked car. Tony Lee rode back to Butthole and
Veronica's after the Meat passed out on the couch. The guy who
was sick was still on the front lawn and people were still looking
at him.

When he was inside Tony Lee went hey, did Christi come by?

Butthole was standing at the fridge looking in it for munch-
ies. He stared at Tony Lee, he was so stoned on weed and acid
he didn't seem to know who Tony Lee was or what he was being
asked.

Tony Lee found a girl he didn't know in his closet tangled
up in a mass of blankets on his mattress and laid down next to her
with eyes closed, the exhaustion overcome by the sparkling electric
dream. Tony Lee muttered convulsively and didn't sleep. With the
clarity of reality, he saw Christi overexposed with his erect cock
filling her mouth. Glisten of wet, saliva strand or come. She stared
into his eyes lying on him with hands on his belly, in wide, cracked
open daylight. Then a twisted tubing space station worm with air-
line oval windows. Zooming in, a specimen crawling across a glass
slide, translucent venal branchings pink, which left a trail of clear
protoplasm scum. His eyes were open or not.

Going out to find the sun high at eleven in the morning and
finding with surprise that the sick guy who had been lying in the

yard was still there, but breathing. Tony Lee went back to the unknown girl, sleep flesh angel in white, he woke her with rubber fingered touches.

—some rainy day Tony Lee came into the print shop drunk, stuffed the paper in the wrong direction and passed out. His head lay on the work bench sideways when Alvarez came running up to the press, ringing with the alarms and buzzers of a massive paper jam. He grabbed Tony Lee under the arms, dragged him to the back door, threw him out.

When Tony Lee woke up in the back alley it was raining. Water washed black in the night and though he didn't remember anything he knew he was finished. He walked home and fell asleep with his clothes on.

—used and borrowed equipment filled the practice room at Roxanne's. Against one wall Tony Lee had a large half-stack amplifier, the speaker towers of Sammy-san's PA were crammed in two corners, black microphone cable, crackling hum, timely squeals when the control board knobs were turned too high; they held their ears screaming turn it down, turn it down! The bass amp was next to the mattress covered windows, throbbing 18-inch Celestion metallic thump-bump, they played the whole set one song after the next no pause, only twenty-five minutes long.

Roxanne tapped with a stick on the snare drum rim: Tock.

She went you know we're gettin' pretty tight.

Tony Lee went yeah.

Sammy-san thumped his bass.

Then Roxanne started a four-count beat and Sammy-san picked up, Tony Lee did a climbing arpeggio pattern based on an old *AC/DC* riff he knew and at the bridge they broke into a sort of cacophonous thrash, then went back into the climbing arpeggio distortion mush, a new tune.

Suddenly the Meat rushed into the practice room making a commotion and holding a cold six pack of beer.

He went hey stop, stop for a second stop.

They went what?

Like, I just got through talking to the manager of Raul's on the phone. I told him I go man we got this band together it's really good. He goes oh yeah, you play original don't you? I go sure, for you original punk only. Then he goes well I need to have a couple more auditions next week, you know. So I go really? And he goes yeah man come down on Monday at eleven and lemme hear what you got.

Roxanne slammed her cymbals and blasted the drums screaming, Tony Lee thrashed his guitar and Sammy-san thump-thumped. The Meat picked up the microphone, switched it on, and screeched his loudest screech. Then they broke into a cover of a *Fear* song, a favorite for all the times, *More Beer*

Tony Lee guitar punching chords and Roxanne the Drummer—

Then opening up and slamming them down, all six, because Bald Peter and Butthole were there too. Then shouting for more beer – but they didn't have anymore money.

—fat Mr. Zedenko sat across from Tony Lee reviewing his application, frowning, or it was something else, a kind of mild confusion. Tony Lee couldn't tell.

Mr. Zedenko wore thick horn-rimmed glasses and was bald on top but still had a ring of hair around his head, and he had extraordinarily fat jowls, pouting red lips, his glasses pressing into the plump skin above his ears. Mr. Zedenko: *Far Side* comic strip man, with a tie.

Mr. Zedenko went I see you've never done this kind of work.

No, I haven't.

And how did you find out about this job?

A friend.

Mr. Zedenko stared.

Well, it gets pretty ugly in there sometimes. Since you've never done this sort of work before I think I'll take you on a trial basis for a few days. If you can stomach it, fine. If not, I understand.

Tony Lee thought he could stomach it.

He went no problem Mr. Zedenko. It will be no problem.

Can you start tonight?

Yes.

Mr. Zedenko led him down some hallways into a brightly lit room with operating instruments, lights, an aluminum table with gutters all around, big pipe silver to an aluminum box under the table. Then they entered another room. It had a tile floor, three tiled walls, and a wall of body drawers. Tony Lee knew them from TV shows. The air was cool, smelled of potent chemical cleaners. Tables with extra big rubber wheels stood around . One of them was occupied, the occupant covered with a heavy rubbery sheet. Mr. Zedenko watched Tony Lee carefully.

Tony Lee was unmoved.

Mr. Zedenko went here is were you will work most of the time. There will always be a pathologist on duty and usually another assistant. You will have to clean the bodies, but only when you are told to do so. Sometimes the bodies can't be touched for evidentiary reasons.

Clean the bodies?

Mr. Zedenko nodded his head.

He went but *only* when told to. If you do it when you're not supposed to, that could get you thrown in jail. You don't want to be thrown in jail, do you Mr. Lee?

No sir.

That's right. Anyway after the autopsy it can be the worst part for a beginner like you.

Tony Lee thought he could stomach it.

He went it's no problem.

Mr. Zedenko nodded his head. Well, come on then.

They wheeled the occupied cart into the room with the operating instruments. Mr. Zedenko helped Tony Lee put on some protective clothing.

Keeps the juices off of you, Mr. Zedenko explained. Then he cackled.

When Mr. Zedenko jerked the cloak from the gray naked body Tony Lee remained, still, unmoved. Nausea hit him first when they moved it to the cleaning table, somehow heavier than he'd expected, Tony Lee accidentally knocked the cart away from the table and the head fell back mouth open, face pushed into Tony Lee's crotch.

He puked briefly into the aluminum sink. Water filled his eyes and he wondered if he was fired. He looked at the deflated body on the table and washed out his mouth.

Mr. Zedenko went hey, it happens.

Then they started washing the body. Once he was doing something active again Tony Lee discovered that it was not so disgusting. He turned the body and Mr. Zedenko sprayed it with a hose. Tony Lee began to think that he really would be able to stomach the job. It paid six dollars an hour to start.

—Victor Hitler cruised in his Lincoln Continental. Up and down the streets he looked for his boy. His boy, he thought. And what could be done with him. It had really gone too far, weeks having passed, no word, no sign, not even a call. The houses of Hyde Park flowed past slowly and Victor Hitler kept his eyes open. There were nice houses, trash houses. He cruised slow past the white trash houses. Piles of broken belongings heaped on porches, grass needed trimming, hedges clipped, vines arranged. Victor Hitler shook his head looking at the trash.

He said to himself what kind of people are these?

In driveways of houses that needed painting he saw smashed up rusty automobiles from previous decades. Victor Hitler could not conceive why Tony Lee had deserted their proper, orderly environment in exchange for decay.

It doesn't make any sense, muttered Victor Hitler. This is just trash, plain white trash.

He turned a corner at Ave C and 45th, cruised over to Ave D, and resumed his slow cruising vigil in the other direction. Back and forth he crisscrossed through the neighborhood and found nothing, saw no trace of any punks anywhere. Once he stopped at a wiped out house with hard rock pumping out the windows. He knocked on the door, pounded. Nobody answered and frustrated, driven away by the blaring music, he retreated to his car.

Victor Hitler cruised down Duval. At 31st he had one last whim, and a house caught his eye. It was completely revolting. A sagging wooden porch peeling paint chips with brown weeds sprouting up all over the yard. On the porch, two punks sat on a torn up couch. Victor Hitler parked and got out. It took all of his willpower just to approach them. They saw and stopped talking, stared in awe at the approaching fifty-year old man who was wearing a button down shirt, tie, and permanent press slacks. He looked like Hitler with the same kind of moustache and comb over, but it was gray. The man held himself erect and stiff.

Victor Hitler quit a few paces from the porch. He went good afternoon.

The punks stared at him eyes open wide.

Victor Hitler went listen, you wouldn't happen to know someone named Tony Lee, would you?

The punks looked at each other.

The man-punk, who was Butthole, went no, I don't know any Tony Lee.

The woman-punk, who was Veronica, went that's right, we don't know anyone named Tony Lee. How come you ask us?

Victor Hitler went well, he likes to associate with people, well, with people who dress like you.

They stared at him. Victor Hitler stared back.

Together, they didn't say anything to each other.

After a while Butthole shook his head and went sorry, we just don't know him.

Victor Hitler nodded.

He went well I'm sorry to have bothered you then. Have a nice afternoon. Then he walked back over to his Lincoln Continental, got in, and drove away, feeling like he needed a shower.

—in the morgue Tony Lee worked with a crazy assistant named Eric. Everyone said he was crazy, that he belonged in the nut house. Eric liked to watch through the window when the coroner showed unidentified bodies to people. He took some kind of perverse pleasure in the first look of recognition in the people's faces.

It's not the tears afterward, Eric explained to Tony Lee, it's the change that occurs in the face, the abrupt change in expression when they realize that somebody they loved or knew is in the drawer.

Usually it was quiet, one or two bodies a night at most. Tony Lee started bringing music books with him, books about guitar technique, or sometimes he would read detective stories. He was in the middle of one when they brought in the murder victim. It was in a bag and the guys who brought it shook their heads and went man you better have some gas masks. The body had been found in some woods outside of town, it had been there for several weeks. When they unzipped the bag, everyone in the room threw up but Eric – even Mr. Zedenko. Half the remains washed away with the worms.

After it was over Tony Lee went into Mr. Zedenko's office.

Mr. Zedenko looked at him and knew he would have to find a replacement.

Tony Lee went I'm sorry Zedenko, I can't stomach it.

Mr. Zedenko nodded. He pointed at a chair and went sit down.

Tony Lee sat down and Mr. Zedenko opened a desk drawer. He took out a bottle of whisky and two glasses, poured them each a drink.

Mr. Zedenko went that's the worst I've ever seen. I was impressed with you tonight, though, Mr. Lee. Sure you can't stay on with us? I'll give you a raise to seven-fifty an hour.

Tony Lee downed the rest of his whisky and looked at Mr. Zedenko.

He went Zedenko, I'm starting to dream about dead bodies. I like my bodies pretty, I like bodies in action. These bodies just lie around ugly. They stink up the place. I can't stomach it anymore.

How about 9 an hour?

Tony Lee thought about it for a second.

No, I'm sorry.

The head of Mr. Zedenko nodded.

He went I understand.

He poured another shot of whiskey for Tony Lee. They talked for a while, then Tony Lee left. Mr. Zedenko was a good sort, but Tony Lee did not say goodbye to Eric, who was in the refrigeration room, pretending to clean out the empty drawers so he could sneak looks at the bodies.

—in a car in a parking lot somewhere in the dark, Chuck leaned his head back, mouth open, cock spasming come.

He went uhhh.

After a bit the head of Christi appeared, they mingled briefly intertwined limbs, then he wanted to go.

She went no, not yet.

He went all right.

She went let's talk.

Okay.

Then they said nothing. Christi straightened her blouse and skirt, waiting. Chuck lit a cigarette and cracked the window, smoke floated out into the night. He stared through the windshield, bored.

Christi went well?

Well what?

Well, don't you have anything to say to me?

No.

What the hell do you mean, no?

I just don't have nothin' to say is all.

God damn, what a bastard.

Christi opened up the glove box, took out a bottle with some quaaludes inside, took one. Chuck eyed the pill, watched it disappear into her mouth, the jump of adams apple plunge into stomach.

He went hey, it was your idea to park here and fuck.

We didn't fuck.

Oh man, whatever. Listen, I gotta go to work now.

Fine. Why don't you drop me off at my house. At least I know where to get some real action.

Chuck started the car and went hey, what do you mean?

A glint from his earring registered on Christi's retina. She remained for a moment silent till Chuck nudged her rudely.

Hey, what do you mean?

Christi went I mean drop me off at my house. This is just too much. I give you a blowjob and then you ignore me. Tony Lee wouldn't ignore me.

Chuck said nothing, threw his cigarette out the window.

Christi went so you don't give a shit?

Nope. I don't give a shit. I really don't.

Fine, neither do I. At least Tony Lee can get it up more than once a day.

Ah fuck you, Christi.

That's exactly what Tony is gonna be doin' to me soon, Chuck bastard-bitch fuck.

Without reflection Chuck threw his hand out and it slapped hard Christi's face, which gave way in a yelp.

Then him driving shifting through the gears, and Christi fuming mad and at the next stoplight jumping out, purse swinging mightily in the air, screaming at Chuck and slamming the door closed, and when the light turned green he accelerated away and regretted going out with her at all, now he'd lost a 'lude and some dope.

Christi walked toward home, pissed off, needing some kind of real fix, staggering figure in the dark.

—through the long hall the vacuum whined, pitch alternating with directional change, brushes whirling, battering compressed carpet fibers fat. Behind it the guiding hand of Mom, her hearing occasionally the clicks and thracks of mud particles flicking through metal tube before being sucked into the dust bag firm. In the long war against disorder, holding her own, occasional thoughts and regrets, she was thinking about her runaway.

Her husband had said: He didn't runaway. He left.

She didn't agree. Turning at the end of the hall, she saw the head of her daughter poking around the corner, from the top of stairway, and with a finger flicked the vacuum into off.

Her daughter went mamma, Tony's on the phone.

With a short yelp then she ran down the hall and stairs, held the receiver to her ear.

Tony?

Hey mom, it's me.

Tony, are you all right, my god, where are you? We've been worried sick.

I'm okay. I'm staying with friends.

Tony, when are you corning home?

Hey, don't worry. I'll be by when things cool down. But I don't live with y'all no more, anyway. Just called to say hey, I'm all right.

But Tony we've been so worried. Your father's been looking for you everywhere.

Hey, no need. I'm working and living. Anyway, I'll be calling again, just wanted to let you know I'm not dead, that's all.

But Tony, what about your future?

Listen, I'm good. I love you. Talk to you soon.

Mom heard Tony Lee hang up.

—a light flicked on and from above, Christi's face stared up, hair tangled across indented pillow, skinny bone arm trailing off to one side; under and over her eye socket was blue, puffed. She was high.

Something new, zooming in to see: A detail at the elbow pit, tiny little dots, tracks of injected dope. Her eyelids drooped but she could tell she was waking from her long nod.

She wanted Tony Lee; to do it now with a man she loved. This was a feeling for her, not alone. Dry and crisp etched by hopping sand on the windy salt flat, under a sun. Seeing this coming down from dope and the rather long twist of a bird running low and there, bushes, a rabbit skipping away. Then at the club bouncing, to make bad boys pay, with skin head.

Chuck, moved her mouth.

Sitting up she went you fucker.

Then lying down and making up lies, to lie, together with the warmth of Tony Lee, who wouldn't ignore her. Chuck for dope speed and 'ludes, Tony for softened cum, do you love, in touching.

The phone was ringing.

She picked up and went hey Tony, I miss you.

Wow how'd you know it was me?

You wanna come by?

She left the phone on the bed, uncradled, face up. An hour later she covered the beep-beep-beep with pillow and blanket; the door she'd gone, the door is open for you. But he was already there. Sitting on the side of the bed, Tony Lee reached down, kissed her on the head, the nose, the lips.

He went hey, what happened to you?

Chuck beat me.

What?

He wanted to fuck, but I wouldn't let him.

Tony Lee brought her a glass of water.

For a long time they talked, she was rambling about how much she dug him, which was true, and maybe about him moving in, her luring until she had him, she felt, there, where she wanted to be taken, slow, with feeling maybe of love.

Not brutal.

Tony Lee kissing around her bruised eye. Pushing covers away in the early evening, pulling cotton on flesh, up, between a moist fold, and after, them breathing in ease, looking out at a purple-red sky, soft, soft as the sunset fading.

—the Meat nudged Tony Lee on the arm, held out the joint. Tony Lee frowned, but grabbed it, took a toke, tried to hold it but right away hacked out two lungfuls hard. Then he coughed even more and fell backward.

The Meat started laughing.

Oh man, look at all that wasted weed floating away!

Tony Lee went man, fuck this shit. Y'all are crazy. I'll just stick with beer.

The Meat took the joint back.

They stared out over the lake. The water was dark, a beautiful glassy brown. In the middle of the lake a boat sped past, the motor humming mild.

The Meat went hey, you're not gonna get married or something crazy, are ya?

Tony Lee laughed.

Oh man, she's a great chick, but I'm not never gettin' married. Her roommate moved out, that's all. She asked me if I wanted to move in. I told her sure.

So she's pretty good, huh?

She's too good. She likes to fuck like a man likes to fuck. The only problem is that she does a little too much crank. She can't get to sleep. She's bouncin' on the bed all day and all night.

The Meat was quiet and stared at the big rock they were sitting on.

He went dude I need to stop the speed.

Tony Lee went what?

The Meat went you know I changed, right? Well, it's 'cause I was doing speed. That shit just changed me and made me aggressive. But I don't need that anymore. I don't need to be crazy aggressive, I've got what I need inside me already.

He thumped his chest and went I'm a *new man!*

Tony Lee laughed.

The Meat went I'm thinking of going straight edge.

Tony Lee went what's straight edge?

No more drink and no more drugs. Just the music. No more nothin' but music.

Tony Lee went dude.

The Meat went really man it's too much. Too much beer too much wine too much booze, weed, crank, and coke. And then this Christi girl you're all in love with and shit.

Tony Lee went what? What about her?

Dude she is like all up in dope. I mean, I've got a friend has seen her OD once but they pumped her stomach or something at the hospital and she lived.

Pumped her stomach?

Hell I don't know what they did. They saved her.

Tony Lee was still.

Man you need to see if you can reach her or something. That ex-boyfriend of hers Chuck got her into dope and she's been doing it more and more.

Tony Lee went how do you know?

The Meat went Roxanne and Suzy told me.

Tony Lee didn't know what to think.

So he went hey, this summer's been the most fun ever, the very best one ever.

The Meat roared.

He went our band man. One fuckin' punk summer.

Tony Lee went hell yeah.

The Meat slapped Tony Lee on the shoulder and went hey man let's go.

Tony Lee went all right man.

They climbed down from the rock, picked up their bikes, and rode.

—the manager of Raul's, Mutton, finished rolling a joint in the office. The desk was a mass of receipts, a ledger and calculator buried somewhere underneath, cigarette butts, a filthy ashtray. Mutton had a sagging face of wrinkles and pockets of fat. His long graying hair hung down in oily straggles and his belly button showed from under the hem of his T-shirt, which didn't completely cover the curve of his gut. Tufts of hair grew from the bridge of his nose. Mutton walked out into the club, sat down in the middle of the room. On the stage he saw the Meat and his band waiting. They stood calm, almost sullen, most the kids who auditioned were nerved-out. He struck a match and lit his joint, took a healthy hit. Then he nodded his head, somehow spoke without exhaling much smoke.

What did you tell me your band name was?

Sammy-san went *meatpiston*.

Mutton couldn't help laughing and blew out the rest of the smoke he'd been holding in. Then he coughed.

Goddammit. You made me waste a hit.

When Mutton stabilized he leaned back smiling and went all right let's hear it.

The first song was one Tony Lee had at last written, *bodies inaction*; the Meat snapped to attention at the mic, raised his fist and shouted:

ONE TWO THREE FOUR

And the whole band came in playing fast, the Meat belting it out:

Working night shift
Sleep all day
Cold strangers come
They slide away,
They're bodies!
Bodies in the drawer!

They bring them in
We tag their toes
It's not so bad
That's how it goes
They're bodies!
Bodies in the morgue!

This mom comes in
I pull the drawer
My son she screams
I say no more

They're bodies!
Bodies in the drawer!

Just bodies!
Bodies in the drawer! Just bodies!
Bodies in the morgue!
The band stopped and the Meat screamed:
EINS ZWEI DREI VIER
BODIES!

Mutton took a deep hit from his joint, looked at the band, all the members standing stiffs.

He nodded at them and went listen, that's not too bad. Play some more.

Mutton sat through their thrash unmoved. On the stage they were sweating and after each song they looked out at Mutton and he nodded his head and they would look at each other again and not know if he liked them or not. After the last song the Meat had big sweat stains under his arms. In the silence they could hear amplifier hum and Mutton stood up.

He went well that wasn't bad at all. Y'all want some beer, don't ya?

The Meat went hey, sure.

Mutton knocked chairs and tables out of his way as he went behind the bar. He looked over at them they were still on stage.

He went hey, what the hell are you still standing there for. Come on down, you got yourselves a gig.

—there on the floor of the bathroom the syringe, a shiny spoon concave up, rubber tubing, and a knocked over candle. Tony Lee watching Christi on the floor limp
       arms to her sides
         hands unclenched
He went hey Christi ah Christi what'd you do to yourself Christi?

After a while she was up and stumbling around she went oh man oh man oh man. Then she was lying on the bed and Tony Lee was really pumping heart. That was when he looked at her arm and saw small traces of tracks.

—days later Tony Lee told the Meat and Suzy Creamcheese about Christi on the way to see the *Violent Femmes*.

He went hey Meat, Christi's into some real shit.

The Meat went like, I told you. What now?

Like, I came home and caught her after she'd shot up. All the stuff was still in the bathroom and she was lying on the floor all limp and shit.

The Meat went like, man, like, that's crazy shit. She's gonna hurt herself. I mean, you know, that's how Janis Joplin died. She OD'd shootin' up all by herself.

Silence for a while then the Meat went what are you gonna do about it?

Tony Lee was upset.

He went man I don't know what to do about it.

Suzy cruised down the riverfront road while they talked and turned onto Second St. heading toward the concert hall, the Liberty Lunch bashhouse for slam.

Tony Lee went like, she says she's not hooked. She says she just tried it a few times.

Suzy Creamcheese went really? I don't believe that shit. She's OD'd before. I saw it. Is she getting dope from Chuck?

Tony Lee went yeah I guess that guy Chuck.

—from his new job at a student bookstore Tony Lee had money and paid for their tickets. Inside the Meat bought two pitchers and they downed them. They saw Butthole, Bald Peter, and Roxanne. They talked to them and listened to the opener *Big Boys*, slammed, sweated, felt good. After the set they drank more beer. Then Butthole wanted a joint so they went outside and he lit up in the dark, away from the people going in and out.

The Meat waved it away when Butthole offered.

The Meat went straight edge.

Butthole went what? You just drank a pitcher.

One thing at a time dude.

They all laughed.

Suzy went hey maybe y'all should've brought your stuff and set up on the sidewalk and played. That's sorta how the *Femmes* got started I heard.

Tony Lee went ha!

The Meat went hey, really, that's how the *Femmes* got discovered.

Tony Lee went yeah?

Sure, like, they set up on a corner down from where the *Ramones* was playing and Joey Ramone saw them and got them a contract.

Then Butthole went hey!

He pulled on Tony Lee's arm, pointed, and went hey, look over there.

They all looked and saw Chuck on the corner opposite talking to Christi. They were arguing and Christi suddenly swirled around and walked away. Chuck was yelling at her and as she walked away she raised her arm, the middle finger pointing up skinny at the sky – *fuck you Chuck!*

Tony Lee went man, I hate that dude.

The Meat went yeah, let's go talk to that asshole.

Tony Lee and Butthole followed the Meat across the street and approached Chuck, who was still cursing Christi and telling her how much money and how many blowjobs she owed him. They came up quick and the Meat grabbed him from behind: One arm around his neck and the other snatching Chuck's right arm and twisting it up behind his back so that Chuck yelped and stopped shouting at Christi.

Tony Lee grabbed Chuck's other arm they pushed him down the street, Butthole following, Chuck struggling yelling what the fuck assholes what the fuck all the way across the street corner and further down and then into a small alley and behind a dumpster.

The Meat hissed into his ear don't struggle motherfucker I'll pop your god damn head off.

Chuck clutched at the massive forearm around his neck, opened and closed his mouth and tried to breathe clenching his teeth; his spittle coming out in gobs and running down the Meat's forearm.

Butthole went let him talk.

The Meat released pressure and Chuck went what the fuck,

man?

The Meat went we got words for you.

Tony Lee went you're a sorry motherfucker.

Chuck muttered something that came out as a hiss. Then he managed to articulate: Fuck you assholes. I've got friends you don't want to know. Christi is just an addict slut. Don't get yourselves into deep shit because of her.

The Meat went oh man Christi's an addict all right *but because of your skinny ass.*

The Meat twisted a little more on Chuck's arm.

Chuck cried out in pain.

He went go ahead, kick my ass. Christi's a goner anyway.

Tony Lee got angry and punched as hard as he could into Chuck's belly.

Hooooh.

He punched three more times: Hoooh, hoooh, hoooh.

Chuck's head drooped and Tony Lee was breathing hard.

Butthole went I think you knocked the air out of him.

The Meat dropped Chuck to the ground.

Tony Lee went you sorry motherfucker beatin' up on Christi and shit. And Tony Lee feeling adrenaline and violence he'd not known kicked Chuck in the ass because he needed to.

Fucker.

They all stared for a moment then Butthole went we'd better get out of here.

The Meat went okay.

Tony Lee wanted to spit on Chuck but he didn't.

They ran out of the alley and ran around the corner and across the street, shouting, and they went back into Liberty Lunch and listened to *Add It Up* being played right there loud and clear

    bop-up sing-along tune

       they slammed around the stage

      with the rest of the crowd

    adding all of that shit up

and a bunch of other shit too

—day after day and week after week Christi, poor long body skin, curled around the bedpost on the floor when Tony Lee would come home from practice. Or on the bathroom floor fetal ball. Paraphernalia like, all over the place and she told him she'd knocked it all down nodding out. Tony Lee, bending over drunk to see if she could get up off the floor with his help. Around her thin rib cage he placed his hands and lifted her onto the bed.

Tony Lee got a beer from the fridge and cracked it open. Then he put it down.

Fuck that, he thought. *Maybe the Meat is right: Straight edge.*

Instead he made some tea and sipped it in the white rocking chair looking at his girl, with her droopy eyelid gazing back, not seeing him. Outside no moon, lamp light mercury silver on the street, buzzing soft. She'd even lost the lust, the hot heat to fuck. The curved wood blades of the chair creaked as his legs pushed back and forth, back and forth,

And Tony Lee went like, man Christi, this is gettin' to be too much. You gotta' stop this crazy shit. But Christi was out and said nothing.

—noises from the crowd, a shout and bustling, Tony Lee and the Meat, Sammy-san and Roxanne near the stage, talking to Mutton.

Mutton went just jam out like crazy. You should play your whole set, but stretch it out, okay? Twenty-five mintes is too short.

The Meat went okay.

Mutton had a pitcher and poured them all a beer. Here's to the first gig.

Hey!

They tipped up and slammed down. Mutton went back to the primitive sound board as they got on stage and geared up. From in back Mutton gave a thumbs up.

The Meat tilted his head back and roared into the mic. The crowd hooted back, they were right up near the stage, for Tony Lee a spangle of lights and impressions, thunks of last minute tune watching meters settle, the crackle of Sammy-san plugging in with a replacement cord, sweat in the hand.

People whistled.

Hey, they shouted. Hey!

The Meat facing them all, then staring at Tony Lee, face turning to smile and a laugh. He went ah, fuck it,

Shout.

ONE TWO THREE FOUR—

and blitzing out punk power they blasted a jam

coordinated through sixteen channels

and Tony Lee twisting sideways, seeing then slice across the back of Sammy-san, bass strap thick, and upside down flashes of cymbal spun into long shiny wires of guitar string moving, guttural scream, coagulate grains in pulsing heart tubes, face of the Meat in his eyes, straining.

Out in the black bustle to and fro, hair, chains and cuts, the cheapo lights above twisting through colors automatic. They were on. Tony Lee felt the hard pound, thomping and thudding through big speakers, concussion from above in concentric rings of burning punk.

—in response to their frenetic set, the crowd cheered and shouted hell yeah, hell yeah, give us some more!

But they didn't have anymore and agitated, wandering afterwards electrified through the room. Lots of people hitting them on their backs, bumping shoulders, saying hey, like, hey, y'all kicked ass.

Through the speakers coming fuzzy into ringing ears Tony Lee could hear the *Ramones*, inter-set music entertainment while waiting for the next band *Beat On The Brat*

Near the stage a slam.

And Christi was yelling at him, Tony Lee, let's slam too!

All right!

Then they were at the edge of the floor pushing in with elbows flying up, catching blows to the ribs and stomach but it didn't hurt it was fun. They plunged into the center and already the wave effect thrust them back and forth. Somebody fell down and got trampled before the tune was over. Whoever it was limped away holding his knee and the next tune, the *Sex Pistols* hard core jam, Bodies,

They were covered with sweat after two songs. Panting, they went back to their table and the pitcher of beer. They slugged it down and Christi grabbed Tony Lee's leg.

She went hey it was great! Everyone said you were great! And that was how Tony Lee always remembered Christi.

—Tony Lee was outside relaxing with one foot cranked up behind him leaning against the wall of Raul's, and these three UT college dudes walked past and stared at him, scared. Tony Lee smiled at them but said nothing. They didn't say anything either, but one of them kept looking back at Tony Lee. He was dressed as some kind of surfer dude and was about the same age as Tony.

So Tony Lee said hey, you should come check out the scene!

The dude paused like he wanted to come back and go into Raul's but his friends grabbed him.

They went naw man that place is dangerous.

Tony Lee laughed and went back inside. When he came back to the table Christi was talking to a girlfriend. The girl smiled at Tony Lee and leaned over to Christi, whispered in her ear. Christi smiled real big showing teeth shiny. The teeth were bright against her black lipstick. Tonight she had on all black too and Tony Lee liked that she had even painted her fingernails black. Her pale white skin and peroxide blond hair contrasted with her black clothes and made her look wicked. Sitting next to Sammy-san it was like black and white, and they held their arms right next to each other's and laughed.

Sammy-san went wow, that's cool. People should think that's cool.

Christi went I know, right?

And she leaned over and kissed Sammy-san's cheek.

She went you're hot, Sammy!

Tony Lee was taken-aback, but Christi had been talking about a threesome lately. Since Christi thought Sammy was hot Tony Lee figured maybe she was trying to get something going. It sort of bothered him, but sort of didn't. It was all part of her mystery.

She leaned over to Tony Lee and whispered in his ear: Baby, I'll be right back. Maybe I can have some extra fun tonight?

Her eyes were so full of life right then, completely the real Christi not the heroin demon whose eyes held no life at all. It made Tony Lee happy to see her like her old self.

Tony Lee went I'm gonna get us some more beer.

Christ and her friend went to the women's bathroom and Tony Lee went to the bar and scoped-out all the girls. He looked for a beautiful girl who had a shaved head that showed up sometimes at Raul's but he didn't see her tonight. The bartender brought Tony Lee a pitcher and when he got back to the table Christi was already sitting there.

Tony Lee went hey, when do the *Big Boys* play?

He didn't know but Christi had done dope in the bathroom. She was a little spaced and didn't react. Christi's friend came up, squeezed in between Sammy-san and Christi and leaned into her and closed her eyes, smiling.

The *Big Boys* came out and started jamming. Tony Lee saw the slams and wanted to partake but Christ was kind of falling asleep at the table and he figured if he left she'd fall over.

He went Christi hey Christi.

She opened her eyes but they didn't really seem like she was seeing him.

Instead of answering she smiled and put her head down in her arms folded on the picnic table where they were sitting.

Tony Lee thought maybe she was just like really really sleepy.

She looked truly at peace and it contrasted with the music blaring out so loud, it was weird but Tony Lee decided it was all right and she was good and he was good and so was the music.

Sammy-san looked concerned and he went what's up with Christi?

Tony Lee went ah I think she's just sleepy – maybe passed out from too much beer. She'll be okay.

—they finished a pitcher and Sammy-san went and got another. The *Big Boys* stopped playing and some people came over and told Tony Lee and Sammy-san how much fun they'd had listening to them and asked them all kinds of questions.

It was weird that people wanted to talk to them just because they'd played music. But all the attention felt good. The Meat was over in another corner of the bar and a bunch of people were talking to him and he was making all kinds of gesticulations. After awhile when all the people left Tony Lee put down his beer and lightly shook Christi's arm.

He went hey, Christi.

Christi didn't move. She didn't react at all.

Tony Lee lifted her head up. He looked into her eyes which were mostly closed and glazed over.

What's wrong Christi?

He shook her a little but she didn't react.

Tony Lee looked at Sammy-san and went maybe we should take her back home.

Sammy-san went okay.

Together they lifted up Christi, each putting one of Christi's arms over their shoulder and slowly walking out, trying not to draw attention but Christi looked sort of like she had been put on a cross and was being carried to her crucifixion.

They walked Christi toward her car which was down the street a little ways, and she seemed to get limper and limper and was really going down fast, but people walking by, cars driving past on the street, oblivious, the world in flashing colors swaying around them now and black sky above, flashes of skin.

Tony Lee and Sammy-san set her down against her car. Her legs and arms were bent funny and her skirt twisted. They let go of her and she just slumped right over.

Sammy-san went shit what's wrong with her?

Tony Lee went I don't know. He bent down and tried to wake her up. He shook her arms and then got in her face and tried to make her see him, he opened her eyes with his fingers, blank stare—

He went Christi, come on baby wake up Christi.

Tony Lee felt the sharp jab of panic.

He went shit – her keys are always in her purse. We didn't bring her fucking purse.

Sammy-san went maybe I'll go back and get it
        well maybe you should go back and get it
            I mean you're her boyfriend and all
            I mean if they see a black dude
        taking a girl's purse
        leaving with it
    I'll be completely fucked man

But Tony Lee wasn't hearing Sammy-san's truth.

He tried to revive Christi some more but nothing doing. And

that's when it finally hit him.

He stood up and went shit Sammy! I think she's OD'ing, I think we got to get her to the hospital!

Sammy-san was scared suddenly and entered defense mode. He went no man, she's all right, she's just ... she's just tired.

But Christi looked like she might already be dead.

Tony Lee went no Sammy – you gotta go call 911.

Sammy-san hesitated, eyes-wide, looking down at Christi.

Tony Lee pointed
   at the Burger King
      and went go dude go
     go call an ambulance
    she might fucking die
   and Sammy-san ran
  and Tony Lee freaked

—like this bad dream it seemed forever before they heard a siren coming; Tony Lee crouching next to Christi who was lying down on the sidewalk, people walking past trying to pretend nothing was happening until this one sorority looking girl busted loose from her friends and came hurrying over.

She went hey what happened?

Tony Lee looked at her scared and went I don't know. I don't know what's wrong with her.

The girl bent down and went let me see what I can do, I'm a nurse.

You are?

She ignored Tony Lee's question and leaned down to check Christi's pulse and listen to her breathe.

The nurse looked up at Tony and Sammy-san and went do you guys know if she took anything?

What do you mean?

I mean like some kind of drugs or something?

Tony Lee blurted she might have taken heroin.

Okay went the nurse and more people were standing around watching and coming over to look and then the ambulance was finally pulling up. The ambulance dudes got out and came over and the nurse turned to them and started talking.

She went I think this girl is overdosing. These guys say she might have taken heroin.

Like it was completely routine the dudes from the ambulance shook their heads up and down and went okay, we'll take her to Brackenridge.

Tony Lee felt helpless as the ambulance dudes got a stretcher out and did all of the things that they do: Strapping her limp body to the gurney and putting an oxygen mask on her and then he remembered his job at the hospital morgue and he got really fucking scared.

He stepped forward and went is she going to die?

The ambulance dudes ignored him.

They loaded her in, and then one of the guys got into the cab and one stayed in the back with Christi. He looked at Tony Lee as he stepped out to grab the door.

Tony Lee went hey, I mean, is she going to die?

He went I don't know, kid.

Then he shut the door and the ambulance pulled away with its lights on and the siren blaring.

—the Meat and Butthole and Roxanne ran up, with Bald Peter huffing along behind. Suzy was still inside Raul's.

The Meat went what happened? What the hell happened?

Tony Lee went Christi might be overdosing dude.

Jesus man. Where'd they take her?

Sammy-san went Brackenridge.

Shit, let's go.

Roxanne went yeah, let's go.

The Meat shoved Christi's purse into Tony Lee's stomach.

He went take Christi's car. We'll take Suzy's and meet you over there. He turned and ran back to Raul's to get Suzy.

Tony Lee fumbled in Christi's purse and couldn't find shit, and wondered how she found anything in there, but at last in some hidden side pocket found keys. Tony Lee jumped in the driver's seat and Sammy-san got in the other side.

Sammy-san went dude, can you drive a standard?

Tony Lee went no.

—at the hospital Tony Lee and Sammy-san didn't know where to go or what to do so they went through the big glass sliding double doors under the lighted sign that in big red letters announced its job:

EMERGENCY ROOM

Inside there were a few people sitting around watching *The Jeffersons* on TV, and a big desk with a big woman sitting behind it. They walked up to the desk but she didn't look up at them right away. A phone on her desk rang and she grunted and picked up the receiver; she listened with her eyes looking over some clipboards, which she flipped a couple of pages on.

Then she went okay, that'll be fine. I'll take care of that.

She hung up and seemed to see the boys for the first time, and a puzzled expression came over her face as she looked them up and down. She even leaned forward a little to be able to see them head to toe.

She went hmm. You boys have an emergency?

Sammy-san went well ...

Tony Lee butted in.

Our friend got brought in. They said she might be overdosing on heroin. We want to go see her.

As Tony Lee explained this, the emergency room double doors opened and the Meat, Butthole, Roxanne, Suzy, and Bald Peter came in.

The lady at the desk did a double take.

She went well, I guess I really haven't seen it all, have I?

The Meat came up and went what about Christi?

Tony Lee went we're asking about her now.

The lady went well what's the name of this person who got brought in here?

Tony Lee went Christi. Her name's Christi.

The lady paused, cocked her head a little, and smiled kindly.

She went and ... her last name?

Everyone was quiet. The lady raised her eyebrows, and she reached her hand up and pushed on the back of her Afro a little.

Suzy Creamcheese went Callantine. Christi Callantine.

The lady nodded and she glanced down at her clipboards.

Any of y'all related?

Tony Lee blurted out I'm her boyfriend.

She looked at Tony Lee, watched him for a moment, and then shook her head.

All right. Let me tell y'all something: There ain't no Christi Callantine on my lists here. But I just started like five minutes ago. There's been several ambulances come in and out last hout or so. I'd like to help y'all but—

Tony Lee blurted out can we just go look for her?

Her face relaxed with empathy and she sighed.

Listen, I can't just let anybody into the hospital to roam around looking for Christi Callantine. She isn't even registered. Ain't none of y'all family?

No ma'am. Just friends.

She deflated a little.

I'm sorry y'all. No Christi Callantine has been checked-in through the ER.

Just then the automatic doors to the emergency room opened and a woman and a man came in. The guy staggered over toward them and right in front of the desk he dropped to his knees, put one arm on his side, lifted the other arm pleading at the lady behind the desk, and wailed in pain.

He went I think I'm dying of a heart attack!

In that moment a nurse came out of the double doors that lead further into the hospital and she looked the guy over as he continued to wail and then he fell onto all fours and cried out again, reaching out toward the nurse.

He went it hurts inside, it hurts inside!

Then he howled in pain almost like a dog.

The nurse looked at the desk lady and went it's probably kidney stones. Let's get him in.

Again the man cried out in tremendous pain, but stood up and lurched after the nurse through the double doors.

The lady at the desk looked at the woman who'd come in with the guy.

You with him?

I'm his wife.

All right, let's get his information.

What are they going to do for him? the wife asked.

They'll get him some morphine back there so he'll stop screaming.

The desk lady looked at Tony Lee.

She went morphine. It's the only thing you can use to stop kidney stone pain. Heroin's almost the same thing, 'cept heroin's not very clean. Sorry I can't help you kids. You can come back tomorrow. If we know about some Christi Callantine by then you can leave your names and we'll see if she wants to see you or not.

—dawn spread her colors across the heavens, and Tony Lee was lying in Christi's white bed looking at everything in her room: The posters the desk the clothes the papers the unpaid bills all the furniture and he kept taking her pillow and smelling it. The pillow smelled like Christi. He hadn't slept all night, even drinking a full six pack couldn't make him pass out. He'd seen some pills in Christi's medicine cabinet, but no way.

In the afternoon he found a crumpled paper with a number scrawled out and a name: Chuck.

Tony Lee was going to burn it but decided he might need it.

He was wishing she was there with him but not sure what was going to happen and why, and he called the hospital like fifteen times asking about her but they finally asked him to stop calling. There was no Christi Callantine. Later he ate food and it was starting to get dark; a whole day had passed doing nothing and not knowing, exhausted yet not sleeping. Nobody knew.

Finally it was darkening again he didn't bother to turn on any lights and he was asleep but didn't know he was asleep. He was dreaming about flying a small plane, looking for a place to land, and then a warning device started buzzing. He couldn't figure out what the warning was for. The only thing he knew was that he wasn't a pilot and didn't know how to fly so why was he at the controls of an airplane? Then he started to realize the buzzing wasn't a warning device in an airplane but was actually a telephone ringing.

Tony Lee opened his eyes and looked at the phone; behind that he saw the digital clock: The time was 11:11.

Tony Lee had dread. He didn't want to answer so he let the machine answer; he heard Christi's sweet voice explaining that she wasn't home but to leave her a message. Then it beeped.

He heard the Meat, crackly voice.

He went Tony, pick up man. I know you're there. Pick up.
Tony Lee picked up.
Yeah?
Silence, which made Tony Lee want to hang up.
The Meat went listen man.
Tony Lee didn't want to listen.
Don't say it man. I don't want to hear you say it.
The Meat hesitated, but he was not a fuck-around kind of guy.
He went Tony, Suzy Creamcheese says that Christi didn't make it.

—Tony Lee went outside and sat on the small grassy slope of the house where he used to live with Christi. It was like she was still there. He threw himself backwards, stared at the empty night sky. Tears and anguish and nothing and cicada chirp.

He closed his eyes and thought it's like she's still here. It's like she's gonna come home.

His hands tore clumps of grass out of the ground and he could smell fresh dirt.

He saw her lipstick smeared and her body limp when the ambulance guys took her away. He smelled his fingers which had been touching the pillow and they smelled like Christi and grass and dirt and he cried more. He could not think she was a body. He could not handle thinking of her maybe with Mr. Zedenko and Eric. Tony Lee got up and walked down the street and didn't register the things.

All of them went past and he didn't care.

He walked and walked and kept on walking he didn't know and it didn't matter.

When he came to again he was all the way downtown.

It was so fucking hot he was totally soaked in sweat.

But Tony Lee didn't know that and didn't really see where he was, he saw her angel white skin, tint of blue.

Then later he realized he was sitting on a loading platform be-hind a warehouse across a street by the MoPac bridge over Lamar, staring at the night sky hearing crickets feeling the oppressive heat.

He was waiting for a train.

Under the bridge cars thumped past, back and forth across the

Colorado River. What difference did it make?

He didn't know. Maybe he should lie down on the tracks. Maybe he should run. Maybe he should go ask about Christi at the hospital. There could be a mistake.

This isn't real, he thought.

Then he said it out loud: This is not real.

He could still feel his hand in hers, when he wanted, thinking of the first time at Suzy's, and all the times since; he could hear her infectious laugh as though she were sitting right next to him kicking her legs up in the air and him running his hand up the leg and over her body and then kissing; and it was like she went into the ambulance but if he kept trying to stop the door from closing, if he'd just kept trying she'd still be here. But he didn't and the door had closed and now she was gone.

—in the distance Tony Lee heard the deep rumble of freight train.

He saw the black tracks shiny rail top. A switch track clacked and moved, mechanical pressure. The train came closer and he quickly hopped down off of the loading platform and walked right up to the tracks.

He went fuck this and fuck that.

Tony Lee watched the train come slowly north across the river, over the bridge he'd seen a thousand million times and it had meant nothing but now it was delivering everything. He wanted to open that door.

The train dieseled slow and powerful. He watched it arrive on his side of the river and how it followed a slow curve until it was headed straight at him.

He had an urge.

Tony Lee went you gotta be strong, dude. You can do it because who cares anyway?

The wheels rolling, the diesel cyclops-light shining on him and the tracks, it rumbled louder and louder and he could feel the energy of it coming from the ground up, shaking his whole body through his feet and legs, right up through him to the top of his head.

The engines screeched and squealed ringing bright over Lamar bridge, wheels clack-clacking over thousand-ton switch track black. Three engines rumbled. He leaned forward, toward the first engine, screaming, he was screaming Christi!

The train driver blared the horn.

Tony Lee grimacing and leaning in as far as he could.

Christi!

Bared teeth waiting for it.

Then the first engine went past inches from his head and then the next and the next after that. No matter how hard he tried he could not make himself lean into the passing train. When all the engines were past it was the box cars a-rolling, jostled and banging. Incapable he stepped back from the grade and picked up a big jagged rock and hurled it.

PONG

It bounced off the steel side of the car and the sound echoed.

Tony Lee went what the fuck kind of world is this?

He screamed it as loud as he could: What the fuck kind of world?

The rocks bounced off boxcar metal. Tony Lee hurled again and again, hard as he could.

Finally the whole train had passed. He was still breathing. He still had all of his parts.

Tony Lee leaned his head back on its hinge, gazed at the heavens.

He heard the train wheels sing and wail against unyielding strips of black iron track. He listened, looked, and saw the caboose light snuff out in the distance; he stood until the train was totally gone, echo of deep rumble and panting; Tony Lee was out of breath sweat. Then it was just crickets, their rhythmic chirp, and the soft whirr-thump of cars going under the bridge like nothing had changed. But he was full in the heat of summer, one punk summer.

Tony Lee turned, crammed his hands in his pockets, scuffed down the street in the dark.

www.ingramcontent.com/pod-product-compliance
Lightning Source LLC
Chambersburg PA
CBHW052143220626
47052CB00005B/1173

bodies
in action to:

Raul's Club

FEAR

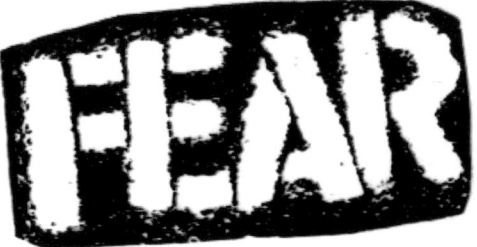

HUSKER DU

I Don't Care About You

Beef Boloney

BLACK FLAG

Gimme Some Action

SEX PISTOLS

RAMONES

VIOLENT FEMMES

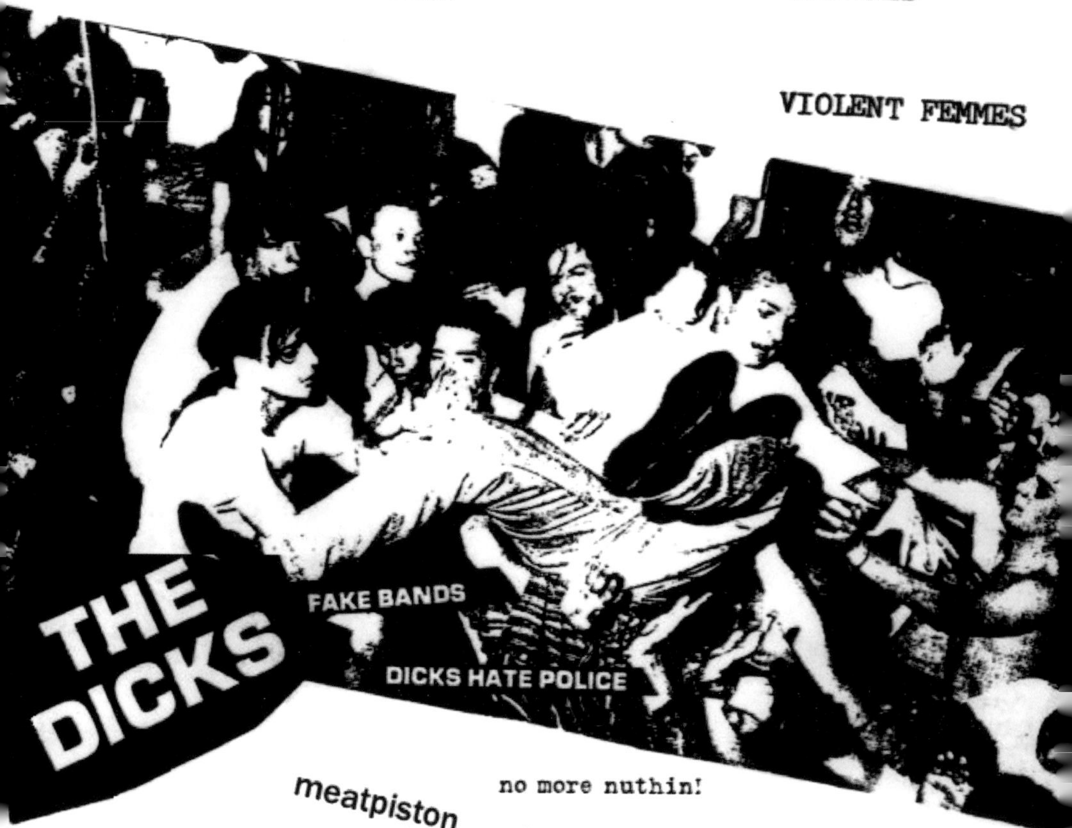
THE DICKS
FAKE BANDS
DICKS HATE POLICE

meatpiston

no more nuthin!

i want your face

korn kabob

bodies

Experimental Chapbook Press

ISBN: 978-1-7364310-0-9

US $9.99

50999

9 781736 431009